By STEPHEN OSBORNE

NOVELS

DUNCAN ANDREWS THRILLERS
Pale as a Ghost
Animal Instinct
The Scarlet Tide

Pop Goes the Weasel
Rat Bastard

Wrestling With Jesus

Published by DREAMSPINNER PRESS
http://www.dreamspinnerpress.com

Rat
Bastard

Stephen Osborne

Dreamspinner Press

Published by
Dreamspinner Press
5032 Capital Circle SW
Suite 2, PMB# 279
Tallahassee, FL 32305-7886
USA
http://www.dreamspinnerpress.com/

Rat Bastard
© 2014 Stephen Osborne.

Cover Art
© 2014 Anne Cain.
annecain.art@gmail.com
Cover content is for illustrative purposes only and any person depicted on the cover is a model.

ISBN: 978-1-62798-556-7
Digital ISBN: 978-1-62798-557-4

Printed in the United States of America
First Edition
March 2014

To my sister-in-law, Sue
a fellow dog lover

Chapter One

I DON'T know if you've ever been ordered to appear before the Tribunal of the Holy Office of the Inquisition, better known to one and all as the Spanish Inquisition, but if you have, you know how I felt when I received a summons to meet my stepfather in his den at the family homestead just outside of Rockford, Illinois.

If, and it would have to have been in a previous life, naturally, as the said Inquisition was established in 1480 and wasn't officially abolished until 1834, you were brought before Torquemada to get your hands slapped or be burned at the stake—depending on how the roast duck was settling in his stomach that day—you understand. The butterflies in my stomach had started off that morning dancing a jig, but by the time I pulled my Corvette into the drive at the appointed hour, they had progressed to a debauched orgy not seen since the days of Caligula. I had chomped on a couple of Tums to try to quell the little bastards, but the butterflies sneered as the antacid entered their domain and went on partying.

I was met at the door by Rita, the woman whom my mother employs to clean the house, cook the meals, and generally do everything so that my mom could enjoy her sherry while pretending to be an artist. Rita was a saint, but then you'd have to be to deal with both my mother and stepmonster on a day-to-day basis. Ma isn't a bad sort, but she was absentminded at the best of times, had trouble with flatulence, and nearly always had a dab of paint on her nose. The last item was always a puzzle to me, as she rarely got any on her canvases. She spent most of her time before her easel with her thumb stuck out, doing some measurements in her head of the apple or whatever she was attempting to paint, and then she'd have a sip of sherry. Once the sherry was down, she'd go back to eying her thumb. Then it would be another sherry. You get the picture.

Mom, though, was a breeze to get along with, as long as you could follow her train of thought. The stepmonster was another story. Jasper K. Dollings was a publisher by trade. Don't go to your bookshelves to see if you have anything foisted upon the public by his firm, though. You won't find any. Daddy Dollings only publishes stuffy, tedious books that, I assume, are for people who have difficulty sleeping. He hates me with a grand passion. We were never what you would call chummy, but after he discovered his stepson liked to sleep with other boys, the animosity was cranked up several more notches. And when Rita greeted me upon entering, looking like a funeral director saying hi to one of the bereaved, my hopes didn't exactly soar.

"Hello, Mr. Patrick," she said.

Nearly everyone calls me Weasel, in no small part because my last name is Weasley. Friends all call me Weasel. My boyfriend, Tony, calls me Weasel. At least, I hoped he was my boyfriend. More on that later. My mother calls me Weasel. Hell, even some of my professors call me Weasel, usually in conjunction with the words "You're late again" or "And what's your excuse this time?" or "If you had a brain in that skull of yours, you'd know." Two people I've never been able to get to address me by the preferred nickname are the stepmonster—a lost cause, I suspect—and Rita. I can't even get Rita to drop the Mister bit. I know she means well, and she says it out of respect, but it makes me feel like I should be wearing a suit and working at a bank, eying frightened clients over half-moon glasses and saying "Now, about this loan application…."

I gave Rita a peck on the cheek, something she pretends to dislike but always makes her blush. "Hello, dollface. What's new?"

She touched her cheek where my lips had recently been doing their business and furtively looked around to make sure no one had spotted the action. Satisfied she wasn't going to be fired for making out with the son of the household, she said, "Nothing's new, except your mother has taken up painting nudes and has models coming into the studio and standing there for hours without a stitch on while she stares at them and—"

"Really? That old dog. Still, you can't blame her. Having seen the stepmonster in all his glory, she probably feels the need to be reminded that the human form isn't as bad as all that. Good lookers, are they? Maybe I should poke my head in and—"

I started to move for the hall, but Rita held up a restraining hand. "Mr. Jasper is waiting for you up in the den."

"Ah, yes." Thinking about male models in the buff had temporarily forced the reason for my visit out of my mind. "In a good mood, is he?"

Rita looked glum. "When I saw him earlier, he was smiling."

That was bad. When an ogre of Jasper Dollings's caliber sports a grin on his mug, someone is about to land in the soup. People like him only smile when plotting the demise of the good and worthy, and if they're having a good time, it's because they know they're about to pull the wings off some unsuspecting fly or kick a Girl Scout and steal her cookies. If Daddy Dollings was up in his den grinning like a tiger being offered a slab of meat, it didn't bode well for yours truly. I took a deep breath and squared the shoulders. "I guess I'd better go up, then. My will is in the safe in my bedroom, under my Spider-Man comics and my old Pokemon cards. Wish me luck."

"Good luck, Mr. Patrick." She said it like she meant it.

As I mounted the steps to the second floor, I tried to think what horrors awaited me. It couldn't have anything to do with college. My grades had actually improved over the last month, as I was trying to prove to the world and my Tony—mostly Tony, though… sorry, world—that not only was I devilishly handsome but smart as a whip as well. Nope, couldn't be that. My trust fund? No, it couldn't be that either. Much as he would like to be in control of my money, my trust fund was in my mother's keeping.

Perhaps a word is needed here about my money. Technically, I have oodles. Practically, I have none. My father died several years back while eating a banana and riding a motorcycle. If you have any doubts, I'm here to inform you that the two do not go together. His passing left my mother quite a tidy sum, and she used it to get married to the dastardly Dollings. My dough was set up into a trust fund, and, for some reason known only to my banana-loving dad, doesn't actually become mine until I reach the age of twenty-five. Most people would have gone for twenty-one, but Pop held out for the quarter-century mark. Mom, being the trustee, makes sure I get a good allowance, so I can't complain. But, really, Dad, twenty-five? And couldn't the banana have waited?

So, it wasn't money Dollings wanted to see me about. And it wasn't trouble with college, which I have to admit is unusual for me. Let the record show, though, that my slate is pretty clean as far as Rockford College goes. No incidents there that have resulted in messages from the dean that stop just short of requesting me to be clapped in irons and thrown into the brig. I hadn't been in trouble at school since the last place I got thrown out of—Purdue University. Did you know they frown on their students swimming naked in the school fountain? You'd have thought that, if they had such strong feelings about it, they'd have posted a sign warning against it. Personally, I think my naked form improved the ambiance measurably.

I arrived at the Spider's Den, so all would soon be known.

The door was closed, so I knocked. A bark came from within, telling me to enter, so I did.

It may be that you haven't met my stepfather. If you haven't, consider yourself lucky. History is filled with despicable characters. Attila (head Hun). Hitler ('nuff said). Jack (the Ripper dude). The guy who invented Muzak. These guys are fluffy bunnies compared to Jasper K. Dollings.

The room was dim and lined with bookshelves, which normally would have been a joy, but these volumes were all from Dollings Press, so they were snorers of the first order. The blinds on the window were opened, but even the sun was hesitant to come in and get a look at my stepfather, so it sort of just hovered outside and waited for a better opportunity. The stepmonster was seated behind his desk, all puffy faced and generally looking like a good bowel movement was days overdue. Even though he had asked me to come, he didn't seem pleased with Weasels darkening his doorway. "Sit down," he said gruffly.

I looked first to make sure there wasn't a tack on the chair. It was just the sort of thing Dollings would do. Being evil incarnate, I guess it's hard to overcome one's nature. Seeing nothing that would poke into the Weasel posterior, I sat.

His face couldn't decide whether it wanted to sneer or frown, so it did both. "I suppose you're wondering why I asked you to come."

"I'm all a-quiver with anticipation."

The sneer went away so he could concentrate on the frown, which deepened. "Why don't you talk like normal people? Who the hell says a-quiver?"

Well, I just did, but I thought I shouldn't point that out. I tried a disarming smile, but it was wasted on Dollings. I might as well have been grinning at a hungry crocodile. "I merely meant I was interested to find out what you had to impart."

"There you go again! Impart! Why can't you just say you want to know what I'm going to say?"

For one, I'm of the opinion that there are loads of words in the English language that don't get their fair share of the limelight, and I like to cart them out every now and then, dust them off, and give them an airing. I was about to say something along these lines when he cut me off.

"It's about your allowance. I'm cutting it down. From now on, you'll get half of what you were getting before."

I gasped. "I'm sorry. I could have sworn you said half."

"I did say half."

"But that's impossible."

"Nothing impossible about it." His lips did an odd curl at the ends. On most people, it would be a smile. "I'm cutting your allowance by half."

"But Mom handles—"

"Your mother and me reached an agreement," he said, cutting me off again. His lips did more of their flexing exercises, and his eyes even twinkled. He was enjoying this. "I'm in control of your money now."

I was stunned. I stared at him. His mustache wasn't actually long enough to twirl, but if it had been, he'd have been doing his Simon Legree impression. "But...," I said. It wasn't much of a protest, but it seemed to sum up things quite accurately, so I repeated it. "But...."

"At a loss for words, eh?" The stepmonster welcomed the sneer back.

I thought I'd give appealing to his good nature a try. I knew he didn't have one, but I had to try something. "I'm barely getting by as it is! I can't survive on any less than I'm getting now!"

His eyes narrowed. "I have it on good authority that you've been spending every weekend at the Winston place in Shannon. You eat out all the time, you go to bars and parties, and as for your liquor bill... well, I have to conclude that you're not only keeping yourself inebriated, but all of your disreputable friends as well."

Was he having me watched? How did he know about my trips to Winston Manor?

There were several incorrect facts in his statement. True, I did spend most weekends out at my friend Jake's family home—a huge monstrosity Count Dracula would have gladly called home—but Winston Manor wasn't really in Shannon. It was out in the middle of nowhere, about midway between Shannon and Polo. Goodness knows why the Winston who built the place decided to put it there. "I'm really rich," one can hear him saying, "and I want to build a big fucking mansion and stick in right in the middle of a bunch of cows and cornfields." Maybe he thought it would be a *Field of*

Rat Bastard

Dreams thing. You know, build it and the town will come to you. If so, he greatly underestimated the town.

But Winston Manor had one really great thing going for it: my beau, Tony, worked there. He served the Winstons and their guests their meals and helped out, keeping the place from falling to ruin. Tony and I haven't been together long, and you know how it is when love is fresh and still blooming. You can't keep your hands off each other. We hit it off right away. I admit, at first it was probably just lust. After all, Tony is really, really cute. But we kept on seeing each other, and, while the lust is still there, popping up and saying hi every now and then, we've fallen in love. At least, I think we have.

Being young and having a strong libido, I've had quite a few guys in my bed over the years, but I've never been in love with any of them. I just know I feel differently about Tony. I think about him a lot. A whole lot. And if that's not love, then I don't know what is.

But—and this is a big but—the weekends at the Manor, I must admit, hadn't been all I'd hoped. Short visits, for the most part. Tony seemed to always be working, and when we did get some time together, we seemed to spend it strolling hand in hand on the lawns or playing billiards. And we'd just get to the end of the evening and I'd be hoping Tony would invite me to his room when he'd take me to the front door and give me a good night kiss. Granted, he shared his room with another manor employee, but still, you'd think we could at least neck. So, while Tony *seemed* to be my boyfriend, I wasn't sure.

Another burst of vitriol from my stepfather took me out of my reverie. "So, no more parties. No more squandering money. And no more weekends out of town."

I was a bit on the pale side, but I blanched nonetheless. "What? You can't do that!"

"I can do what I like, you idiotic whelp." Dollings was truly enjoying himself. "I know that you're still seeing that… boy."

Actually, Tony was slightly older than me, so "young man" would have been more appropriate than "boy," but one has to pick one's battles. However, I was so angry that words wouldn't come out of my mouth. I knew Dollings and his cronies at the church he attends had made it their personal mission to generally make life hell for anyone gay. The stepmonster had participated in protest marches at several Pride Parades and gathered outside many a gay bar, holding up signs and shouting, generally while his stepson was within, having a gay old time. So I knew we didn't see eye to eye on the whole man-loving-man thing, but his calling Tony "boy" was hitting below the belt.

Finally I found voice. "His name is Tony." I didn't actually add the phrase "You rat bastard" to the end of my sentence, but I feel it was implied.

"I don't care what his name is. You're not to see him anymore."

I snorted. "Excuse me! Try and stop me!"

The stepmonster leaned back in his chair. "Fine. On your way out, please leave the keys to your car on the desk. Oh, and you'll have to come up with next semester's tuition on your own."

"Car. Mine." There were other words said, but they sounded unintelligible even to me. I got my point across, though, I believe.

"It's in your mother's name," Dollings said, shaking his head in mock sadness. "And we also won't be paying the rent on your apartment."

I looked up, wondering where the ten-ton anvil was that was about to fall and crush me. Let's face it—that would have been the only thing that could have made the meeting worse.

"MOM, YOU'VE got to get him to see reason." I was pulling out all the stops. I was doing the pouting lips. I was giving her the puppy dog eyes. I even threw a little hitch in my breathing into the middle of the sentence to show the depth of my feelings.

Mother, a little spot of cobalt blue on the tip of her nose, rolled her eyes. "Weasel, you know as well as I do that reason and your stepfather have little in common."

Rat Bastard

"He wants—no, demands!—that I stop seeing Tony." I trailed after her as she returned to her easel, after she'd refreshed herself with a healthy swig of sherry. "And he wanted me to leave the car keys, and he said he wouldn't pay for my schooling, and... does he have to be here?" The last bit referred to her model, a rather hot guy with glistening muscles who stood totally stark naked not five feet away from us, posing like Michelangelo's David.

"Of course he does. I'm painting him."

"He's got an erection."

Mom peered over the top of her glasses at the impressive member in question. "Yes, he has. I ask all my models to be erect. I do so hate painting limp ones. They always look like dried fruit."

I arched an eyebrow. "How many penises have you seen?"

"Quite a few, darling. I'm an artiste."

If that's what it took to be an artiste, then I qualified as an artiste supreme. I tried to ignore the model, which wasn't easy. He was even taller than I was, which placed him around the six foot four mark at least, and his pectoral muscles looked like they had hidden weapons inside. I was half worried that at any moment bullets were going to shoot out of his nipples like a machine gun. I forced myself to look away from him. Unfortunately, I glanced at Mom's canvas, where she had painted him, badly, but with an even more enormous and spitting-mad penis than he already had. I looked at Mom. "I can't live on what he's willing to give me as an allowance. I'll starve." I plucked at my T-shirt to illustrate that the Weasel frame was already thin. Any further deterioration in body mass and I could disappear entirely.

"You can always come here and eat, darling."

"Are you insane?" I immediately regretted my outburst, as my mother's sanity was a bone of contention amongst my aunts, uncles, and assorted cousins. But still, eat at Chez Weasley? With the stepmonster at the table? That would be enough to put anyone off their meal.

But wait a moment, Weasel, you might be saying to yourself. You left the previous scene too soon. How did it play out? Did you tell Dollings where to get off? Did you storm indignantly out of the room, vowing never to darken his doorway again?

Not exactly. I may have left him with the impression that I was kowtowing to his demands. As for said demands, he had another bombshell that he'd dropped. It had gone like this:

Dollings: "Do I make myself clear?"

Me: (slumped dejectedly in chair) "Yes."

Dollings: "One more thing. I want you to go out with Cicely Talbot."

Me: (Unintelligible words and gurgling sounds.)

Dollings: "For some reason, she's still interested in you. Call her. Here's her number."

It could be that you're unfamiliar with this Talbot sprout. She's my stalker. Has been since a Christmas party my mother threw years ago for her friends. Cicely had been the only person present that had been around my age, so naturally I gravitated toward her for chatting purposes. After a mere hour in the Weasel presence, though, this seemingly mild young gal suddenly became an octopus, and there were few places on me that didn't get attention from her tentacles. It was only by cunning and guile that I escaped her clutches that night. However, she had dogged me ever since. My mother's sanity may be questionable, but Cicely's was definitely in the loony category. She had tried to get me to marry her on several occasions, and the fact that I'm gay seemed to have little effect on her. After seeing Tony and me kissing, I thought she'd finally seen reason, but apparently that wasn't the case.

But I digress. Back to my spirit being crushed by the stepmonster. Any fly on the wall looking on would have thought I was beaten, meekly agreeing to all of Dollings's demands. However, I was inwardly defiant. The stepmonster might have thought he had me by the short hairs, but he was mistaken. Whatever he asked, I was going to continue to see Tony. I would just have to be more circumspect about it.

I knew why Daddy Dollings wanted me to ask out the dreaded Cicely. First, he could say to his cronies at his church, "See? My stepson isn't a homo. He's dating a girl." But more importantly, this Talbot menace was also a writer who had written a biography of my buddy Jake's Great Aunt Charlotte, a minor political figure in the area, and Dollings desperately wanted to publish the thing. Jake's great aunt, it might be mentioned, had been the owner of Winston Manor. Up until her death, that is.

I filled my mother in on her husband's dastardly schemes, ending with, "And he wants me to go out with Cicely Talbot! Can you imagine?"

"I think you should, Weasel. She's a nice girl."

I had to put a steadying hand on a nearby table, as the room seemed to be whirling. I stared at her, not believing my ears. "For one, she's crazy. And I'm not talking kooky, fun loving, and quirky. I'm talking straightjackets and psychiatrists shaking their heads and going 'Tsk, tsk.' I foresee a future where she'll be locked away in a padded room to protect an unsuspecting populace."

Mom got some paint on her brush and applied it to the canvas. It didn't help. "You're being too harsh, Weasel. She's not that bad."

"She is! But, putting the mad Talbot aside for the moment, there's also the fact that I'm gay."

"No, you're not."

I gaped. "Say what?"

She was pretty involved smearing colors all over her canvas and spoke in a distracted manner. "Your stepfather has been explaining it to me. This is just a phase you're going through. A rebellion against authority figures. So you're not really gay."

I glanced over at the model. "Want me to prove it?"

The model winked at me. I think his penis winked as well. I didn't wink back, as that would have been leading the poor guy on, but I did smile at him. The Weasel of old would have shoved the parental unit out of the room, locked the door, and then made sweet love with the guy, but the new, improved Weasel was dating Tony. Dating just one person was a new experience for me, and I wasn't about to fuck it up. And besides, I think the model guy had a few too many muscles. I don't mind a dude being in shape, but these things can be overdone. When your muscles have muscles, you've gone too far.

He certainly had an abundance of them on Mom's canvas, where he resembled the Michelin Man on steroids. The mater paused to daub more paint onto her brush. She glanced at me and sighed heavily. "Really, Patrick!" When she actually used my name, I knew I'd gone too far. "Your Christmas break is coming up. You won't need much of an allowance when you're not in school."

I frowned. "Actually, that's when I need it the most."

"I'll work on your stepfather. Now, do go away. You're spoiling my concentration."

With a sigh, I prepared to exit, knowing I wouldn't get anywhere if I stayed and further pleaded my case. I passed the model on my way to the door and looked down at his crotch for one last gander. Oh, if only. "Viagra?" I asked him.

He nodded.

"Sorry," I told him.

He shrugged. "She pays well."

Sure. Everyone gets a good chunk of the Weasley fortune. Except yours truly.

Chapter Two

EVER NOTICE how, when you're in a gloomy mood, the sky is often gray and laden with clouds of the darkish variety? It's as if the heavens are saying, "We're feeling pretty low about this as well. We think we'll rain for a bit. Maybe throw in some snow flurries. And don't blame us if you hear some thunder later."

Tony was in town for the evening, which perked me up a little. We went to a McDonald's for dinner and met my friend Caps there. Caps, whose real name is Jake (the same Jake whose uncle owned Winston Manor, where Tony worked), wanted to pay, but I insisted on buying my own food. "I'll have to get used to eating meager meals," I explained. While I still had my allowance, I wanted to be frugal. With a tyrant like Jasper Dollings in charge of my dough, it was only a matter of time before the plug was pulled and I'd find myself sans moolah.

We walked away from the counter with our trays, Tony's and Jake's laden with burgers and fries while mine had one small sandwich and a small Coke. Tony frowned. "Really, Weasel, let us get you something else. That's not going to fill you up."

It wouldn't, but I remained firm. The rumbling in my belly would be a reminder that I had a shitty family. Once we'd seated ourselves and started to dig in, I regaled them with my tale of woe. In the telling, I may have glossed over the model and his erect member a bit. No need sowing the seeds of jealousy when they aren't necessary. Both Tony and Jake were obviously moved by my story.

"What are you going to do?" Tony asked.

I took a bite of my burger. One fourth of it was gone in one bite. I chewed slowly, hoping I could fool my stomach into thinking it was getting more than it actually was. Once I'd swallowed, I said, "Well, I'll have to get a job." By agreeing to a date with the lunatic Cicely and a promise—already broken, but some promises just are meant to be shattered—not to see Tony again, I had gotten the stepmonster to temporarily keep my allowance going, but I was still low on funds. I had nothing to buy Christmas presents with, and I wanted to get something special for Tony. I had no idea what, but it had to be special.

"What?" Jake asked. I was still getting used to thinking about him as Jake, as opposed to Caps. To me, he'd been Caps since that time he'd taken a bunch of us out on the boat his parents had bought him. We'd killed the boat in a day, but the nickname Caps had stayed around for years. Now, though, Jake was dating a guy named Keith and suddenly didn't want to go by his nickname. Keith preferred the name Jake, so Jake wanted me and all his cronies to go along with the notion. Luckily, I didn't have that problem with Tony, who preferred Weasel to Patrick. Who wouldn't?

"Being from a monied family," I replied, eying Jake darkly, "you're probably unfamiliar with the concept, but people get paid for working places. They're called jobs. The chipmunk-cheeked girl who served us at the counter? She's not doing that for the fun of it. McDonald's pays her to take people's orders and, more importantly, their money."

"I know what a job is," Caps—dammit, I mean Jake—said testily. "But what sort of job are we talking about here?" It seemed to me he was purposely waving his french fries in front of his lips before chucking them in, as if taunting me. "It won't be easy to find something that pays well. Most places have already done their Christmas hiring. And you've still got finals coming up."

For once, I wasn't too worried about finals, having done a lot of studying over the past few weeks. Dead People and Dates, or History as some people refer to it, would be a doddle. I had so many dead people and what they did to contribute to society running around in my brain that I was afraid my skull would begin to bulge. Folklore, my favorite class, was going to be an easy A. Calculus promised to be a bit trickier, but a few nights sweating over the books tanked to the gills with Mountain Dew would solve that problem. "There's got to be something I can do over Christmas break," I said.

"You can always work for my uncle," Jake said, his mouth full of semi-masticated burger.

I sat up, intrigued. Working for Jake's uncle would mean working alongside Tony, which would be sweet. "Doing what?"

Jake saw my excitement and immediately threw on a dampener. "Not Uncle Mark. This is an uncle on my mother's side of the family. He runs a bed-and-breakfast down in Byron. It's called the Phantom Lady Inn."

I admit I wasn't as thrilled as I had been, but I was still intrigued. Byron was a smallish town just a ten or fifteen minute toodle down Highway Two. "What would I do there?"

"Not much," Jake said. He took a big slurp of his Coke. Mine had long since done a vanishing act. "The place is tanking money like nobody's business. Let's face it, who wants to stay at a bed-and-breakfast in Byron? What the heck is there to do in Byron, except leave it as soon as possible?"

Tony wiped his lips with a McNapkin. A slight frown showed on his adorable face. Have I mentioned his big brown eyes yet? I could write volumes on them. But I digress. Tony, with his cute frown, said, "Didn't I just read something in the paper about Byron? Some fire or something?"

Jake nodded. "Yeah. Second one in a week. Someone torched a Dumpster, and then yesterday they think the same guy set fire to some poor sod's car."

"Why would someone set fire to a Dumpster? What did a Dumpster ever do to annoy anyone?" I asked.

"Some dude got his car burned up," Jake said, making a sour face, "and you're worried about a Dumpster. Get some perspective, Weasel. Anyway, the police think that it's a firebug. An arsonist."

"Just saying," I grumbled. "Innocent Dumpster."

Wisely, Tony got the conversation back on track. He asked Jake, "What would Weasel do if he went to work at your uncle's place?"

I thought I detected a hint of an underlying suggestion I wasn't qualified for much of anything, but I let this slide. "Yes? Does he need a manager? Someone to fry up the eggs and bacon? Spruce up the rooms and leave a little piece of chocolate on the pillow?"

Jake shook his head. "Front desk. He fired the guy he had working for him. You'd be pretty bored, to tell the truth, Weasel. They really don't have much business."

It sounded right up my alley. "Could I bring my Kindle?"

"I'd say it would be essential. Anything to keep you from falling asleep."

I was still making my way through the works of A. Conan Doyle, and was currently on *The Hound of the Baskervilles.* Getting paid for reading Sherlock Holmes stories seemed too good to be true. "Why did your uncle fire the last guy?"

"He was watching porn and jerking off when some guests came in."

"Probably covered on page seven of the Employee Handbook. He should have studied it with more care."

Jake promised to put in a word for me, and we finished our meals. My stomach wondered why the hell I was teasing it, saying, "Seriously now. Where's the rest?" We put on our jackets and dutifully tossed our detritus into the trash receptacles and made our way to the exit. Outside, the sun had begun to peek around a cloud, and it seemed like it might not be such a bad day after all when Tony, who had been walking slightly in front of me, suddenly stopped, causing me to have to do some fancy footwork to avoid collision.

Rat Bastard

"Shit," he said, staring at some guy getting out of a gray pickup.

I wasn't sure why Tony was compelled to mutter epithets under his breath at the sight of some random guy, so I sized up the dude, using the Sherlock Holmes method. Generally Holmes liked to analyze guys while sitting in front of his fire at his Baker Street lodgings, long legs stretched out and pressing his fingertips together while wearing his mouse-colored dressing gown. I had no fireplace handy, and mouse-colored dressing gowns were notable for their absence (by the way, Doyle, if you mean dark gray, just *say* dark gray, as *no one* uses the phrase "mouse colored" except you), but I gave it my best shot.

Okay, Tony must know the guy. One rarely says "shit" when spying strangers, unless the stranger seems in some way dangerous. And this guy, while he was muscular and solidly built, didn't look immediately threatening. He was about our age, early twenties, and was wearing cowboy boots, tight jeans, and a heavy jacket. His brown hair was cut very short, and he had ears that stuck out a bit. He was, I assessed, a typical farm-boy type. While Rockford was a sizable city, it was surrounded by small towns and farm country, and there were tons of this sort of guy around. I bet his pickup's radio was tuned to a country station and he owned at least one shotgun.

And there the Sherlock Holmes method kind of petered out. Holmes could seemingly pull rabbits from hats by spotting a tattoo that could only have been done in China, or by seeing that the subject's cuffs were worn, showing that he had done a lot of writing recently, but this guy wasn't so obliging in visual clues. He had beady eyes, though, and a bit of a sneer to his lip. From this, I deduced he had a bit of a temper to him. I was to learn in mere minutes just how accurate that deduction was.

He spotted Tony, and the sneer became a brief smile before going back to a sneer when he took in Jake and me as well. He approached us with a bit of a swagger to his gait—that kind of walk that says "Yeah, I work out and could bench press you *and* a couple of your friends and not break a sweat"—and stopped a few paces in front of Tony. He nodded.

"Hey," he said.

"Hello, Gates." Tony looked like he wanted to be elsewhere.

Gates stuck his hands in the front pockets of his jeans, indicating he wasn't going to just walk around us and go into the restaurant. He wanted to chat. "I've called you and left tons of messages. You haven't answered."

Tony looked down at the pavement. "You know the answer, Gates. It's over between us. It has been for quite a while."

Ah. This Gates fellow was gay. The Sherlock Holmes method doesn't much rely on gaydar. Not only was he gay, but I surmised he was once Tony's boyfriend. Tony and I hadn't actually gone through the "who did you use to date" thing, but I was surprised I hadn't previously heard about this Gates. Something like, "Oh, Weasel, by the way, I used to date some muscle-bound country guy with an unlikely name" springs to mind.

Gates narrowed his eyes. He didn't have huge peepers in the first place, so there wasn't a lot to narrow. "You don't mean that."

"I do." Tony kicked at a pebble. "I'm sorry."

"What we had was special," Gates said. It came out kind of gruffly. He obviously needed to work on his sweet talking.

His manners could have used some overhauling as well, as he then grasped Tony by the arms and pulled him closer. Tony, being an average-sized guy, didn't stand much of a chance. Big, muscle-laden goon yanks person weighing at least forty pounds less, and the lighter guy is going to move. Simple physics. Tony didn't like it, though, and neither did yours truly. I stepped forward.

"Excuse me," I said pleasantly but firmly. "That's my boyfriend you're manhandling."

Gates glared at me as if seeing me for the first time. He looked back at Tony and then at me again. Unable to make up his mind, he then returned to Tony. "You're dating *that*?"

Rat Bastard

I squared my shoulders. This Gates had gone too far. Grasping Tony in an unseemly manner and insulting the Weasel looks demanded action. There were three of us, after all. I had half a mind to stomp on the guy's foot and then yell for the three of us to run for it. And Jake, being the slowest, would have to get caught by an angered bull elephant. Bad for him, of course, but sometimes you have to take one for the team. I was just about to stomp his right cowboy boot when Tony shook himself free.

"I think we've said all we need to say," he told Gates.

Gates was, it seemed, the sort who liked to have his own way, and when he didn't get it, he wanted to fight. He turned to me, a snarl on his lips. "So you prefer this beanpole to me?"

"Weasel," I said.

"What?"

"The beanpole," I explained, "is known as Weasel. Not my actual name, mind you, but it might as well be. You see, my—"

Gates didn't seem interested in the Weasel nomenclature. He poked a finger into my chest, which halted my sentence. "I'm going to be watching for you," he said through clenched teeth. "And I suggest you watch for me, because the next time I see you I'm going to beat the tar out of you."

I tried to look nonchalant, but that's hard to do when a behemoth is bearing down on you. I must say, though, I stood my ground. I retreated not a centimeter, even though Gates was jamming a finger right between two of my ribs. "A bit extreme, wouldn't you say?"

He went on as if I hadn't spoken. "I'm going to beat the crap out of you. And when you're lying on the ground twitching, I'm going to stomp you. Repeatedly."

The scene he described was a vivid one. I may have gulped loudly. "I don't suppose you'd settle for thumb wrestling?"

Gates finally removed the finger from my chest. I was sure I'd have a tiny bruise where his probing digit had been. "Just watch out, pretty boy!"

I noted that, even though he wanted to pummel me until I was a heap on the ground, he still couldn't deny, after he'd taken some time to reflect, that the Weasel looks were pleasing. Gates, having said his piece, stepped around me, shoved Jake out of the way, and made his way into the restaurant. It wasn't until the door had closed behind him that we all dared to breathe.

"Oh, my God," Tony muttered. "I'm so sorry about that."

I turned to Jake. "Thanks for jumping in there," I said sarcastically.

"I was too stunned to move! Who was that guy?"

"My ex," Tony said glumly. "A mistake if there ever was one."

"He does seem to have some issues," I replied. I rubbed my chest. It still hurt from being poked. "Gates, eh? Odd name."

"His last name is Stumpenhorst."

I blinked. "You're joking, naturally."

"I wish I was."

"Gates Stumpenhorst?"

"Yes."

I shrugged. "If you say so. And you dated him?"

Tony sighed. "What can I say? It was a small town. Not much to choose from. And I do have a tendency to go for the bad boys. I didn't expect to run into him, though. I thought he was still in the slammer."

"Jail? Gates has done time?"

Another sigh. "Yeah. Assault and battery. He likes to get into fights."

"He should join a roller derby team or something. Work out those aggressions in a civilized manner, with other apes. Who did he assault and batter?"

Sigh number three. "Some guy. I was just talking with him. You know, kind of harmlessly flirting with. It was at a party. Gates had been drinking."

Rat Bastard

My eyebrows danced a little as I tried to decide to settle the face on astonished or downright perplexed or amazingly worried. "And he beat the snot out of him?"

"This was before I met you."

"Naturally."

"I should have mentioned it. Sorry."

I glanced back at the restaurant door and exhaled loudly. I'd have to be on my guard to make sure I didn't cross paths with Tony's ex ever again. It would be bad enough to be trounced by some guy, but to be trounced by a dude with the name of Gates Stumpenhorst would be adding insult to multiple injuries.

Chapter Three

I OPENED an eye. Something was making noise. I opened the other eye and pointed both of them at the alarm clock. It wasn't making a peep. Something, though, had disturbed the slumbers. My brain suddenly remembered it was Saturday. As I didn't have classes, whatever was trying to rouse me could go to blazes. I pulled the covers up over my head and tried to ignore the thundering.

Finally I recognized the sound as someone banging on my front door. I groaned and slid out of bed, taking one of my sheets with me. I kept it sort of wrapped around my frame, as I was clad only in boxer shorts, and if you answer the door almost naked and it's a Girl Scout selling cookies, it can be embarrassing for both you and the cookie promoter, especially if you're sporting morning wood. Although, I suppose that depends on your Girl Scout. I know some who are pretty cheeky, and they'd have their cell phones out in a flash, and before you know it, your semi-naked form, complete with stiffy, would be splashed all over Facebook and other social media sites.

Luckily, for as soon as I opened the door my sheet slid down my legs and my tented boxers were revealed in all their glory, it wasn't a scout of the female variety but Jake awaiting my arrival.

He looked down at my underwear. "Jesus, Weasel, are you always horny?"

I grunted and retrieved the sheet, halfheartedly covering myself once more. I turned and headed back to the bedroom, knowing Jake would follow. I didn't answer his question, as I assumed it was rhetorical. Of course I wasn't always horny. Occasionally I was hungry.

In my room, I deposited the sheet back onto the bed and grabbed some jeans from the floor. As I was putting them on, I muttered, "What are you doing here so early?"

"It's two in the afternoon."

I looked at the clock on my nightstand. "So it is."

I had spent the previous evening in a favorite watering hole, drowning my sorrows. Tony had to go back to Winston Manor to keep the Winstons fed and generally keep their rambling house from falling apart, so I had been on my own. I had thought a liberal amount of gin, mixed with some tonic water, would make calling the insane Cicely an easier task, but I'd gone a bit overboard on the Dutch courage and had instead stewed myself to the gills. As I found a T-shirt and some socks to wear, my head throbbed abominably, reminding me there was a price to pay for overindulging alcoholic beverages.

It wasn't only the prospect of having to ask out a young woman who should be locked away as a menace to society that caused me to drown the sorrows. My little chat with the stepmonster had made me look at some ugly truths about my life, mainly the fact that it wasn't going the way I wanted it to. Before being browbeaten by the ogre who shares my mother's bed, I had a nagging feeling something wasn't going as planned, but I couldn't exactly put my finger on it. Now I could. And it involved Tony.

Let's face it. The pre-Tony Weasel slept around a bit. I wasn't up to Casanova standards (Giacomo Casanova, eighteenth century Italian dude famous for boinking a lot of women—take that, Dead People and Dates class!), but I had my fair share and maybe more. I always knew that one day I would find someone who would make all that cease, and I wanted it to be Tony. Therein lay the problem. I was used to boffing quite regularly. Now, not so much. Tony lived and worked in a different town, making getting together problematical. Also, his work schedule and my school schedule didn't seem to gel very well. True, I was seeing him nearly every weekend, but that was for eating out at some restaurant or seeing a movie or such. Then he'd have to shuffle back to the Manor and I'd have to toddle back to school. We weren't, to put it bluntly, getting much sack time. And by much, I mean any. Oh, we were smooching like turtledoves, if that's what turtledoves do when they get together, but actual boinking eluded us. And that was bothering me greatly. In a way, Caps—I mean Jake (really, really hard to not think of him by his old nickname.... Damn new boyfriends!)—had been right. I was almost constantly horny. If things kept up the way they'd been going, my right hand was going to be worn down to a nub.

And here's where the Boyfriend Zone comes into play. Bear with me on this. It's an important concept.

Say you meet someone. Someone who makes your heart go flutter. Someone you think may be the one. Is it Insta-love or mere lust? Well, there may be a hint of Insta-love, but most of it is lust. Lust can disguise itself as Insta-love and fool you nine times out of ten. So the first time you get jiggy with this person *doesn't count.* Repeat—doesn't count. Not in a relationship way, anyway. It could fizzle after that one time and turn into a one-night stand or a weekend romance. And there you have it.

But if you want a relationship, you've got to slip into the Boyfriend Zone. There is a time limit between that first time you make love until you do it a second time, and it must be timed perfectly. Do it again right away, and you look just like a horny slut. But—and this is the important bit—if you wait too long, you've missed the Boyfriend Zone. Say you wait a week. Say two. Fine. But three? By then, the love of your life has already said to himself "Oh, that was nice. But he must not really be into me, or we'd have had sex again. So I guess I'd better find someone else. Strange, though. I thought he really liked me. I guess we'll just be good friends." And you go and make your move and wham! He puts the kibosh on the scheme. "Let's just be friends," he tells you, and the romance is officially over.

Tony Turner and I had great sex when we'd first met—well, after some mishaps, such as my stepmonster walking in on us. But we eventually did have a marvelous time during that eventful weekend at Winston Manor. However, after that first meeting, we haven't, I'm sorry to say, had any alone time. Scratch that—alone *naked* time. Alone time where you say things like "Can you move your elbow a little. It's poking me in the ribs" or "Sorry, did that get in your eye?" And if we didn't soon, we'd be out of the Boyfriend Zone. And I couldn't bear that.

I knew Christmas break was just around the corner, and that would alleviate most of that little problem. I'd make sure I spent more time with Tony, especially of the naked variety. But I wanted to do something to show him I appreciated him waiting around for it, so to speak. I wanted to buy him a ring for Christmas.

And, while I'd managed to hold onto my meager allowance, I wouldn't have much left over for Christmas presents. Seeing Jake again reminded me of his job suggestion.

Before I could ask him about it, though, he beat me to the punch. "I was talking to my uncle. The one with the bed-and-breakfast."

"Oh?"

Jake smiled. "He's expecting you to come by this evening for a sort of interview."

I was optimistic but cautious. "He knows I'm a student, right?"

"It came up."

"And my break is only a few weeks long."

"He's aware of that. But you'd still be able to work weekends and a few nights a week if you want, even after school starts up again. He's really just looking for someone to man the front desk so he can go off and potter around the place. I warn you, though. He's eccentric."

"People have said the same of me."

"True."

Jake handed me a card. I eyed it carefully. There was a line drawing of what looked like a large, rambling old farmhouse next to the name and address. "The Phantom Lady Inn?" I asked.

"It's out on Kennedy Hill Road. There's a ghost that haunts the road, or at least there used to be. Uncle named the place after the phantom lady that was supposed to run alongside the road, frightening drivers and generally making a nuisance of herself."

I vaguely recalled hearing something about this specter in my folklore class. "She used to go jogging, I believe, in her underwear. During snowstorms. Quite unhealthy, I would imagine."

"Oh, you've heard of her?"

I nodded. "She hasn't been seen in decades, though, from what I understand."

Jake grimaced. "It would help things if she'd make a reappearance. The possibility of sighting a ghost, especially one nearly naked, might bring a few people to the inn. Like I told you, it's not exactly a popular spot."

"Sounds like just the place for me. I can lean against the desk and Kindle to my heart's content. Study too, of course."

I must admit I also had a vision in my head of sneaking Tony into one of the empty bedrooms and ravishing his naked body, but I kept that thought to myself. I also made a mental note not to bring that up during my job interview. "Mind if I use your place so my boyfriend and I can get jiggy?" might not be a good sentence to use if you want to make a favorable impression.

IT WAS, as Jake had promised, an easy place to find. A quick drive down Highway Two, which ran alongside the Rock River, and then a turn onto Kennedy Hill Road just before Byron. There was a farm or two and a couple of assorted houses, but the Phantom Lady Inn was easy to spot, as it stood on a slight hill. The big wooden sign proclaiming that this was, indeed, the Phantom Lady Inn made it even easier to spot. I pulled into the drive. The inn had once been a farmhouse, as I'd surmised, but had some additions added onto it to make it an even bigger place. It was big, white, and inviting looking.

Rat Bastard

But judging from the lack of cars in the parking lot, not inviting looking enough.

Jake had assured me that dressing up for this interview wouldn't be necessary, but I still felt a bit of spit and polish wouldn't hurt, so I wore a button-down shirt (blue, to match my eyes), black slacks, and the only pair of black shoes I owned. I would have dragged a comb through the locks, but my hair has a way of doing what it wants to do anyway, so I didn't bother. As the weather was on the chilly side, I had my red hoodie on, but that could be ditched as soon as I got inside.

I had bounced up the front steps and was about to enter when something caught my eye. It could be that I was unusually wary, after the threats from Tony's ex (the improbably named Gates Stumpenhorst), but I thought I spied, out of the corner of my eye, one of those plungers they use to set off dynamite sitting by the corner of the house. You know the sort of thing. The coyote was always using them in an attempt to blow the roadrunner sky high, only to blast himself to smithereens. Scowling, I put off my entrance and went over to investigate. It turned out not to be a detonator, which was good, as that would have made me nervous, but a red plastic gasoline canister. I picked it up and heard some of the contents sloshing around inside. I was pondering why the thing was just sitting there by the corner of the house when I heard someone clear his throat behind me. I turned to see an officer of the law standing a few paces away, looking grim.

He was a gruff-looking older guy, the sort you see in movies who walks into a bar on the rough side of town, and all the locals think it would be fun to give him a rough time, and he ends up beating the snot out of all of them, finishing off by dusting off his hands and saying, "And *that's* how we do it in Chicago!" He had a salt-and-pepper mustache, and his hair was close cropped, at least what I could see of it under his hat. His uniform told me he was either a sheriff or a deputy, and his countenance told me he was not a happy one.

"Hello," I said as cheerily as I could manage.

He twisted his mouth around, making his mustache do a little dance. "Can I ask," he said, speaking slowly, "what you think you're doing?"

"Oh. I'm here for a job interview."

I was beginning to think this sheriff was frozen to the spot, as, other than the lower part of his face, not a muscle on him had so much as twitched. He could almost have been a statue standing there. He continued to stare at me with beady eyes. "Oh?"

"Yeah, the owner of this place is an uncle of a friend of mine, and I thought I'd see if I could do a bit of work. Raise some needy cash, if you know what I mean." The guy was making me feel nervous, what with his statue imitation and his gun, which his right hand was much too close to, as if he thought he might have to draw it at any moment.

He shifted his eyes down to the gas canister, which was still in my hand. "And what, may I ask, are you doing with that?"

I held it up. To be truthful, I'd forgotten I was even still holding the damn thing, my mind being occupied with immobile and ominous sheriffs. "This? I just spotted it and wondered what it was. Saw it out of the corner of my eye and thought 'Now, what's that doing there?'"

"So you picked it up?" I got the impression from his tone that he found my story lacking in believability.

I wasn't sure how I could convince him my actions had been innocent, so I just shrugged and said, "Yes."

"It was just sitting there, and you decided to pick it up?"

He was getting the gist of it. "Yes," I said.

Finally, he moved. It was like a spell had been broken. His right hand shifted up to his head, where it did some scratching at his temple. "You know," he said, still in that ponderous way of his, "we've had a lot of trouble with arson around here lately."

"I heard about that on the news." I gulped and set the canister down at my feet, eager to get the thing out of my hands.

"I haven't seen you around town before," he said.

Rat Bastard

Well, he wasn't likely to have done so, as I spent little time in Byron, it not being exactly a hopping town. Mostly I passed through the burg on my way to somewhere else. Not wanting to speak disparagingly about his hamlet, though, I said, "No, I'm not from around here. I live up in Rockford."

He grunted. "I'll need to see some ID."

I fished out my driver's license, and he examined it thoroughly. "Patrick C. Weasley, eh?"

"The C stands for Carrington. People call me Weasel, though."

I thought, now that he knew my name and that I had just happened to pick up the canister and was obviously not a firebug, the ice that seemed to hang in the air between us would melt, but it didn't. His mustache twitched again as he handed me back my license. "I'll be keeping an eye on you, young man," he said.

I was about to reply and let him know I was many things, but an arsonist wasn't one of them, when we were joined by someone else who'd just come around the side of the house. This guy was older as well, with a shock of white hair sticking out from the cap he had on his head. He was thin and had a genial look to him. Seeing me and the sheriff standing together talking in grim tones, he nodded at us each in turn. "Hello, Arthur," he said to the sheriff. "What's going on?"

The law enforcement agent, whose moniker was presumably Arthur, turned to the newcomer and sniffed. "Found this young man here acting suspiciously. Holding a gas can."

I explained to the man in the cap, who I assumed by his air of belonging to the surroundings to be my hopefully future employer, Eric Rivers, uncle to Jake, "I'm Weasel. Jake's friend. He told me to come by tonight."

"So he did, so he did," the man said, nodding. "You needn't have brought gasoline along with you, though. We've got loads of the stuff out in the garage."

"Actually, I just found it here. Sitting by the side of the house."

Officer Arthur's mustache moved around some more. The man must have had an itchy nose. "I caught this young man," he said again, "acting suspiciously. He was splashing gasoline, or so it looked to me, onto the side of the house. I came over to investigate."

"I wasn't doing any splashing," I protested. "See? The cap is in place. I just picked it up and jostled it to see if there was any gas in it."

"Perfectly reasonable thing to do," the man in the cap said. I hoped he was, indeed, Jake's uncle, as I was beginning to like the guy. He was one of those fluffy-minded old dudes. Not stupid, but not given to deep thought if they could help it either. Absentminded. "I'd have done the same," he added.

"And what was he doing at the side of the house with a gas can in the first place?"

"I found it there!" I said.

The man in the cap nodded. "I expect the lawn service I employ left it there. They're always leaving things lying around."

"It's December," Officer Arthur said. "I don't expect your lawn service has been around here for months. And there have been several fires set in the vicinity lately, as you know, Eric."

"Surely you don't suspect this fine youngster of being an arsonist?"

It was obvious by the look in the officer's eye that he did very much suspect me of being such, but he refrained from saying so. He shuffled his feet a bit and said grudgingly, "I suppose not." To me he muttered, "I'll be keeping any eye on you, though." He seemed fond of the phrase.

The officer exchanged a few pleasantries with Mr. Rivers and then departed, heading back to the parking lot, where he'd apparently left his cruiser. Once he'd gone, Rivers patted me affectionately on the shoulder. "You mustn't take Deputy Bradley too seriously," he told me. "He's a good guy—friend of mine—but he's under a lot of pressure from the community to catch his firebug and he's a little overzealous."

"I thought he was going to clap me in irons."

"He did," Mr. Rivers agreed, "have a satisfied gleam to his eye. Still, it's odd that gas can being out here. Wonder who left it there?" He shrugged and seemed to put both the canister and Deputy Arthur Bradley out of his mind. From the dreamy look on his face, I gathered Eric Rivers wasn't the sort to let things bother him. "Anyway, shall we go inside? It's much too cold out here."

"I suppose it would be better to conduct an interview inside," I said jokingly.

"Interview?" Rivers frowned. "Oh, my dear boy, the job is yours if you want it."

"I want it."

Rivers nodded. "One thing, though, that we'd better get out of the way before you sign on for sure. You're not afraid of ghosts, are you?"

Chapter Four

THE VERY next Saturday found me starting work at, technically, the first job I ever had. As a kid, my dad had got a sudden bright idea that I should learn responsibility and told me one summer he'd arranged for me to have a paper route. The idea, if I understand the concept correctly, is that some poor snot has to get up at four thirty in the morning, fold said papers, and then deliver them to the doorsteps of the people who required them. It sounded mad to me, and as the idea of getting up before the sun could even be bothered to rouse itself was beyond my comprehension, I paid Jake to do it for me. Of course, I should have known he'd muck it up, as he was the same dunderhead then as now. He thought delivering newspapers to *specific* houses was asking a bit much, so he just randomly distributed them. My paper route lasted two days.

This job, however, appeared to be custom made for me. I had my own little area behind the front desk in the lobby. I could read, twiddle my thumbs, study, or stand on my head if so desired, as long as I was ready to check in any deluded souls who entered wanting a room. The desk wasn't huge, as Mr. Rivers didn't want a "hotel" look, but there was a counter, complete with sign-in book and a bell and plenty of room for me to spread out my textbooks if I needed to. I had a little stool to sit on if the legs felt like they needed a rest, and there was a radio if I wanted to listen to some music. I found after my first several hours there that these things were necessities to keep from going stark-staring bonkers from boredom, as not a single solitary person came in.

Rat Bastard

I had two fellow employees. Sammy, the cook, who was generally only there in the mornings unless there was some special assignment for him, such as doing up an omelet for the Queen of England if she happened to check in and demanded one before bedtime every night, and Mandy, the housekeeper. I had only met Sammy briefly, but he seemed a nice enough guy. Mandy was in her midtwenties and had loads of brown hair she piled on top of her head in a complex puzzle that must have taken her and an architect hours to do every morning.

I spent my first hour studying. I spent my second hour playing solitaire and reading more of *The Hound of the Baskervilles*. (Watson was spending his nights at Baskerville Hall watching strange lights out on the moors and listening to dogs howling.) Mandy, having pretended to clean rooms and dust, decided a chat was in order, so she leaned against the counter and smiled at me. She was shortish and had an ample frame and chewed gum, which she smacked every now and then.

"You're kind of cute," she said.

I set my Kindle aside. "Thank you."

"Got a girlfriend?" There was a hint of a tiger in search of prey about her.

"Boyfriend," I said.

"Oh," she said, her smile faltering a little. "You're one of those."

"If by one of those you mean one of the fabulous, then yes."

Mandy gave a tiny shrug and let out a sigh. "All the really cute ones these days seem to be gay."

"We planned it that way. All part of our nefarious plan."

"So is your boyfriend cute too?"

"Abercrombie and Fitch models look at him and hand in their cards, saying they can't compete."

She sighed again, deeper this time. "My boyfriend looks like he was molded out of Play-Doh by a particularly inartistic child."

I raised an eyebrow but didn't mention she seemed ready to engage in some major flirting with me but had a boyfriend waiting in the wings. But then, I hadn't met the guy. From her brief description, though, I pictured him as big, lumpy, and smelling faintly of salty wheat while being clothed entirely in muddy primary colors. I shook myself to dispel the image from my mind.

Just then, Sammy came into the lobby, presumably from the kitchen, as he had his chef's jacket on and was holding a spatula. It was well after breakfast time, and he had the air of a man who didn't know what to do with himself, although, as there had been no guests to cook breakfast for anyway, one wondered why the spatula. Maybe he carried it just in case some passing stranger looked like he needed a slice or two of bacon, or to show Mr. Rivers he was, despite rumors to the contrary, a hard-working cook. Sammy was in his midforties and had long, curly brown hair streaked with gray. The glasses he wore had black frames and those tinted lenses that were supposed to get darker depending on how much light there was. These didn't seem to work properly, as they were almost perpetually dark.

"Weasel's gay," Mandy told him.

"Oh?" He looked over the top of his glasses at me. He'd done the same thing earlier when Mr. Rivers had taken me around the place and introduced me to the staff. He didn't actually lick his lips and drool, but I had the impression he was mere seconds away from doing so. "I should have guessed. He moves with a certain grace, like a tiger."

Mandy frowned. "Tigers are gay?"

"No, I...." Sammy let it go. I gathered he spent a lot of time trying to explain things to Mandy and had begun to wonder if it was a lost cause. He turned to me and proffered his hand, which I shook. He held the handshake for much longer than I was comfortable with. "We didn't get to meet properly earlier. I'm Sammy. As you might have guessed," he said, indicating the spatula and chef's jacket, "I'm the cook."

Rat Bastard

I fought the impulse to wipe my hand on my pants. His hand had been sweaty. "I'm Weasel, and I'm the new front desk guy," I said, patting the top of my workstation.

"Much better than the old one," Sammy said. "The guy who used to have your job wasn't very nice. Very morose."

"And he liked to play with himself," Mandy added.

"So I've heard," I said.

Sammy looked over his glasses again, this time at my crotch area. "Adam may have liked to play with himself, but he didn't really have the equipment to put on a good show. You, however, look like you're packing some heat."

I forced a smile, wishing these two would go off and leave me to get on with finding out what Holmes was planning to do with the deadly doggie. "I haven't had any complaints yet," I said, hoping that would put an end to the masturbation portion of the discussion.

It didn't. Both Mandy and Sammy were now checking out the Weasel package. Feeling naked despite being fully clothed, I moved so the lower half view of me was obstructed by the desk. Sammy looked disappointed, but he said, "I bet you could really put on a show."

You couldn't afford the ticket price, I thought. A change of subject was required. "We were talking about my boyfriend before you came in." A good move on my part, I thought. Not only had I shifted the talk, but I'd also pointed out I was already off the market. Bad for Mandy and the lecherous Sammy, but oh well.

"I'd like to meet him," Sammy said.

Why did I have the notion that somehow a three-way was in the back of his mind?

"I need to call him, actually. We've not seen a lot of each other lately, and we need a date night."

Mandy leaned against the counter. "Have him come here! You can cook him a nice dinner, then watch a movie on the big screen TV in the lounge, and, if things go well, you can take him up to your room."

When Mr. Rivers had taken me on my tour, he'd pointed out the rooms on the ground and first floor were for guests, but his quarters were on the third floor, as were rooms for staff. We each had one, just in case things got busy enough (ha!) that we wanted to crash there instead of going home. I'd checked out my room. It was little more than a closet with delusions of grandeur, but it did have the necessary things a bedroom needed, such as a bed. I pondered Mandy's suggestion. There were several pluses. It would be a cheap date, and, as money was being saved for a special present, that was a consideration. It would be convenient. I wouldn't have to use any gas. And things would certainly be quiet. The minuses—I envisioned Mandy and Sammy listening at the keyhole.

The notion of cooking a meal for Tony appealed to me. I'd never actually done much cooking. I can microwave a burrito with the best of them, but most of the culinary duties when I'd lived at home had been the province of the lovely Rita, and on my own I usually opted for eating out. However, I'd seen Jamie Oliver on TV enough that I figured I could whip up something edible. How hard could it be?

I looked at Sammy. "Would I be allowed to use the kitchen?"

"Of course."

"I can run to the store and pick up some steaks or something, and—"

"Dear boy, just find what you need in the larder. If we don't eat it, it just goes to waste. Old man Rivers rarely eats here. He certainly won't notice if any food is missing."

The date was looking cheaper and cheaper. I did some mental calculations. Money saved tonight plus my allowance plus what Rivers would be paying me equaled ring for Tony. "This sounds like a good idea," I said, nodding.

Mandy smiled crookedly. "Just hope the ghost doesn't show up and scare the bejesus out of you just when things are getting romantic."

"Mr. Rivers mentioned that the joint is haunted."

Rat Bastard

"He believes that Phantom Lady lives here."

"Well, the place *is* named for her. If I was a specter, I'd undoubtedly gravitate to a place called The Weasel Inn or The Weasel Arms."

Sammy chuckled. "I haven't seen anything myself, although at night there are some noises that I've never been able to figure out where they're coming from. And Rivers says he's had some things turn up missing. A ring and a tiepin. Things like that."

"A pilfering ghost?"

"He thinks so."

"What would," I asked, "a ghost need with a tiepin? Especially a female ghost known for running about scantily clad? I wouldn't think ties were her style."

"Rivers thinks she takes them just to be mischievous. He's absolutely bonkers on the subject. Well," Sammy said, rolling his eyes, "Rivers is pretty much bonkers in any case, but especially about his ghost. One morning I came in for work and he'd been standing guard all night in the upstairs hallway, waiting for her to appear. He was holding a loaded shotgun as well!"

"Loaded shotguns being a deterrent to ghosts?"

"Loaded with rock salt. Apparently salt isn't good for ghosts."

"Sodium intolerant, are they? Good to know."

There was a little more discussion over working at the Phantom Lady Inn between the three of us, with them filling me in on what to expect, which was mainly a lack of anything to do. They finally moved on, Sammy to head home and Mandy to pretend to do some dusting in the upstairs rooms, which might, to the casual observer, look more like taking a nap. I used my alone time to call Tony and arrange for him to join me for the evening at the inn. It was his evening off, so we agreed he'd arrive about eight o'clock. I got off at six, so that would give me plenty of time to whip up a fantastic meal for the two of us. That settled, I contemplated calling the dreaded Cicely. I hadn't set up my date with her yet, and, as that was contingent to me keeping my allowance, I really needed to do so, but I just couldn't force my fingers to press the number into my cell phone. Maybe the stepmonster would forget that part of the deal. Maybe Cicely had gone to a shrink and was now cured of her obsession with me and was a sane, rational person who I wouldn't mind spending an evening with. Maybe horses play gin rummy with cows when we're not looking.

I decided I'd call when I'd finished *Hound* and Holmes and Watson were back safe and snug in Baker Street. I fired up my Kindle and started to read. I must have been pretty immersed in Doyle's world because I wasn't even aware someone had entered and come up to the desk until they cleared their throat. I looked up with a start. There was a middle-aged woman standing before me, wearing a red coat and a face to match. The coat had a big green Christmas wreath pin on it. The face didn't. She had a big black purse—more of a satchel, really—slung over her right shoulder. I must have been really discombobulated by her sudden arrival, because it seemed to me the bag was moving of its own volition.

"Excuse me, would it be possible to get a room for tonight?"

I blinked. It was only my first day of work, but I'd already gotten so used to the idea that no one ever actually ever stayed at the inn that her request took me by surprise. "I think we've got one available." There were fourteen guest rooms, each one at her beck and call.

"I need quiet. Is this place quiet?"

"Like a tomb."

We went over rates and how long she wanted to stay. She was nearly ready to sign on the dotted line when she paused, pen in hand. "One last question. Do you take pets?"

"Do I take them where?"

"No," she said. The "you dunderhead" was implied. "I mean here at the hotel."

Mr. Rivers had stressed he preferred inn or bed-and-breakfast and wanted to steer clear of calling the place a hotel, but she had ready cash so I didn't correct her. He also hadn't said whether or not felines and canines were allowed, but again, she had money. "We sure do," I said.

"Good." She shifted the bag off her shoulder and placed it on the counter. A little furry head popped out and looked at me. It could have been a small dog. It could have been an uppity rat passing itself off as a canine. "I'll need a room with a doggie bed. Rodney requires his own sleeping space."

"We don't have doggie beds," I told her, "but I could make him up something with some pillows. Or we can wheel him in a cot if he'd prefer that."

She was frosty. "The pillows will do."

I was finishing up the transaction when I realized we didn't have anything like a bellboy. Was I supposed to take her bags to her room? I certainly could. The chances of some other deluded soul coming in and wanting a room while I was away from the desk were astronomical. But I didn't have to worry. Just as Mrs. Kendall (I was good at reading upside down and watched as she scrawled her name in the book) was ready to be taken to her room, Mandy came around the corner. She stopped dead in her tracks when she saw we actually had a customer.

I used a professional voice. "Mandy, Mrs. Kendall will be in Room Seven."

"You're kidding." Mandy realized she said the words aloud and quickly amended them. "I mean, of course. Let me take her things to her room."

She led Mrs. Kendall away, along with the bag containing Rodney and a suitcase that, from the way Mandy had to hoist it, was filled with bowling balls, off to Room Seven. They hadn't been gone for more than a few seconds when Mr. Rivers entered from outdoors.

"How's your first day coming along, young man?" The young man came after a pause, and I suspected he used it because he'd forgotten my name.

"Good. I just checked a lady in."

"Really?" He seemed to think this was unlikely, and I was making it up. He sauntered over and looked at the signature in the sign-in book. "Really? Well, Ferret, it looks like you're good luck. Things are looking up!"

"It's Weasel, sir."

"What is?"

"My name."

"Good for you. That fits you better than the other one."

I thought I'd clear my evening plans with the boss, just to make sure he was okay with the idea. "My shift is over in a few minutes, sir, and—"

"You don't have to call me sir, Wombat."

"It's Weasel, sir."

Mr. Rivers frowned. "If you keep changing your name, things are going to get very confusing."

"I'll keep it Weasel, sir."

"Good. I like that one. What were we talking about?"

"I was going to ask you if I could use the kitchen tonight to cook a special meal for my boyfriend. I've invited him to come here tonight, if that's okay with you."

"Don't see why not. We've plenty of space. Will he be requiring a room?"

"Well, I thought he might stay with me in mine, if you know what I mean."

"Oh, yes. Quite. Have you seen that other young man around? Adam, I think his name was."

"You fired him, sir. I've taken his place."

"Really? Well, good for you! And you're doing a fine job too!" He snaked an arm across the counter to give me a friendly punch on the shoulder. "Well, if you've got your young man coming, you'd better be off. I'll watch the desk for the evening."

I glanced at the clock. "Are you sure, sir? I've still got some time."

"Nonsense. Go prepare yourself. Doll yourself up, or whatever it is you guys do before a date. I can handle things quite well on my own." To prove his words, he came around and joined me behind the counter. He stared at the front door as if he was waiting for the hordes to burst through at any second, demanding rooms.

"Do you want to take your coat off, sir?"

Mr. Rivers still had his bulky orange coat on from his outdoor activities. He looked down, as if shocked to find it on himself. "So I have, Meerkat. So I have." He shrugged out of it, letting it fall to the floor. "Well, that's taken care of that."

I took the coat and went around to hang it on the coat rack by the front door. I took a quick look out the window, seeing that a good December drizzle had decided to fall. Luckily, I wasn't going to be going out. "So it's okay if I use the kitchen?"

"Of course it is, Weasel, my boy."

As he'd got my name right, I took that as a good sign and legged it to the kitchen.

THE KITCHEN of the Phantom Lady Inn was fairly spacious, full of gleaming appliances and pots and pans which got little use. I was expecting the stove to be some antiquated contraption one had to stoke with wood or coal, the house being old, but instead it was a stainless steel job with big red knobs and eight burners on the top. I took a quick inventory of the food supplies and decided I'd keep things simple—as I was by no means a cook—and do a meatloaf, mashed potatoes, green beans, and a salad.

It took me a moment to figure out how to even turn the oven on—there were a hell of a lot of dials on the thing!—and while it was warming up I got to the salad. On the counter I found a wooden cutting board and pulled a load of veggies out and began to chop them. I put everything into a big bowl and then added shreds of lettuce and tossed the contents until I had something which even Gordon Ramsey would have to admit was a salad. I put the bowl in the refrigerator and then diced my potatoes. I got a big saucepan and added them to some water and put them on one of the burners. I turned a knob and figured those suckers could stew a bit while I set about the meatloaf. "This cooking thing," I said aloud, "is a cinch."

I wanted some space to mush my hamburger and breadcrumbs and what have you together on the counter, so I set the wooden cutting board on the stove, on one of the back burners away from my potatoes. I got another big bowl for my meatloaf creation and was digging an egg out of the fridge when my nose twitched. Something was burning. Thinking perhaps I'd set the heat too high on my taters, I turned to the stove to find the cutting board doing an imitation of Joan of Arc.

"Holy shit," I said. It seemed an appropriate epithet. I mean, what else are you supposed to say when you've set fire to a cutting board? I saw right away my mistake. I'd thought I'd turned on the burner under the potatoes, but the one I'd actually turned on had been one of the back ones, where I'd set the innocent cutting board. That's what comes from having too many dials on a stove.

The smoke detector began to chirp loudly. I thought it was a case of too little, too late, and contemplated writing a strongly worded letter to the detector's manufacturer. What, one wonders, is the use of a safety device that sits quietly while a cutting board smolders and scorches and doesn't actually come to life until the thing is in flames? The alarm was loud and hurt my ears, but it would have to wait until I found a way to keep the whole kitchen from becoming an inferno.

I had my oven mitts on and grabbed the cutting board by the one corner that didn't seem to have flames dancing all over it. Remembering that it was raining outside, I quickly hopped across the room to the back door. Flinging this open, I tossed the flambéed board out into the gloaming. It hit a nice grassy spot, and while the rain did it's best to quell the flames, it was up against one hell of an obstacle. Too much fire, not enough rain. The grass around the cutting board started to smoke.

Rat Bastard

I wouldn't say I started to panic, as that would be much too light a word to use for my state of mind. One long moan, nearing scream status, escaped my lips as I rushed around the kitchen looking for a fire extinguisher. They had to have one. Standard issue, I would have thought, especially if the kitchen might possibly be used by someone with no culinary—or stove operating—skills whatsoever. I finally located the blasted thing (by the door, attached to the wall…. Who the hell thought that was a good place to put it?) and, grabbing it, made for the door again.

Outside, standing in the yard over the smoldering cutting board, was Deputy Sheriff Arthur Bradley.

Chapter Five

BY THE time I'd found the extinguisher, the rain had pretty much done the work for me, and the smoking board, blackened like a sea bass that had the misfortune to be snagged by a Cajun chef, seemed to stare up at me accusingly, but not half as accusingly as Bradley was glaring at me.

I held up the fire extinguisher to show that, although it wasn't necessary, I had the situation well in hand. Behind me, the smoke detector was still blasting so loudly that surely folks in Chicago were looking out their windows wondering who was making all the racket. "I kind of set a cutting board on fire," I said by way of explanation.

Bradley did his lip movement thing, making his mustache dance. "Seems like," he said slowly, "every time I run into you, you either are about to set fire to something or already have."

Well, that was a bit unfair. After all, on our first meeting, Bradley had jumped the gun and just assumed I was up to nefarious deeds with the gas can. And here, the only thing that suffered from my incompetence, if you don't count the ears of every person and animal within earshot of the alarm, was the cutting board. Really, I was a hero, keeping the kitchen of the Phantom Lady Inn from going up in flames, but Bradley wasn't going to see it that way.

I was about to let him know the chain of events, but suddenly the kitchen was filled, or so it seemed, with people. I remained in the doorway, but Bradley had shoved past me to make sure the joint wasn't burning to the ground. A scowling and confused Eric Rivers was asking if we had to have so much noise going on. Mandy was screaming at anyone who wanted to listen, asking if she needed to call 911. And, hairy rat of a dog pressed to her bosom, Mrs. Kendall was shouting, "I was told that this place would be quiet! Rodney requires a calm, soothing atmosphere!" The smoke detector, finding that it couldn't compete, fell silent. Or maybe there wasn't any smoke remaining for it to detect. My bet was on the first possibility.

And then a familiar face showed tentatively in the kitchen doorway. Tony, looking lovely as always, was frowning, trying to take in the scene before him. "There was no one in the lobby, and I heard…." Then he saw me and Bradley, in full sheriff gear, looming over me. Well, I was taller, so physically he couldn't loom, but he had a gun strapped to his side. That can give the illusion of a shorter guy looming over a taller one. Tony shook his head. "Oh, Weasel."

It wasn't, it must be said, how I envisioned our dinner going.

"WHEN YOU invited me to come here for a nice, home-cooked dinner," Tony said, much later, "you should have told me there would be a comedy revue as well."

"It wasn't planned."

It was nearing the midnight hour, and we were heading up to the top floor, to my room. The house was—finally—dark and quiet. After going over my story several times, I had convinced everyone, with the possible exception of the skeptical Deputy Bradley, that I had merely burned up a cutting board and hadn't been practicing my firebug antics. Harsh words were said by Mandy, who wondered how anyone could be stupid enough to put a wooden board on a stove, even if he thought that part of the stove wasn't in use, but to be honest I hadn't even remembered putting the damn thing there until it went up in flames. I bet Julia Child burned up dozens of cutting boards in her time. Probably a whole chapter about such incidents in her biography.

We reached the first floor landing, and Tony put an arm around me as we trekked onward. "It's a shame. I like meatloaf."

"The sandwiches we ended up eating, I thought, were quite tasty."

"You made them well. And nothing got scorched or burst into flames."

"I thought cold cuts would be a safe bet."

"And was it your idea to put the cold cuts in between two slices of bread? Sheer genius! I can't believe that everyone was saying you were a menace and shouldn't be allowed anywhere near a kitchen again as long as you lived."

"Your sarcasm is noted. However, perhaps it's a good thing that I'd not planned on attending culinary school."

Tony chuckled and pulled me closer. "Perhaps it is."

We were taking our trudge up the stairs slowly, enjoying each other's company. Outside, the rain had stopped, and, while the moon was still mostly obscured by clouds, there was enough light coming in through the windows for us to see what we were doing without turning on the lights. When we only had a few more steps to go, Tony turned to me, and we paused before going farther. I could see he was smiling.

"I'm glad we've got some time to spend together. Just the two of us," he said.

"Me too." I leaned down and kissed him. Gotta say, it was a nice kiss. What with school and work and what have you, we hadn't even been doing much kissing of late, and it felt good to have his lips against mine and to feel that spark of electricity go right through me and down to my toes.

Midkiss, though, a light shone on us. Temporarily blinded by the sudden shock to the optics, we both put up our hands and blinked a bit. The light was coming from a flashlight, wielded by someone halfway down the third-floor hall.

"Who's that?" a voice asked.

Rat Bastard

I realized the speaker was none other than my boss, Eric Rivers. He sounded a little shaky. "It's me, Weasel," I said. "With Tony."

The light was lowered so it wasn't right in our eyes. "Oh, Weasel. I thought it might have been her."

"Her?"

"The lady."

I thought at first he had been expecting a late-night visitor to his boudoir, but then understanding dawned. "The ghost?"

"Yes." We couldn't see his face. He was just a dark figure holding a flashlight, but I had the impression he was nervous. "She's been out tonight. Prowling around."

Tony and I came up the remaining steps, and Mr. Rivers turned off the flashlight. Once my eyes adjusted to the dimness, I could see he was dressed in a robe and had slippers on his feet. He was just outside the doorway of what had been designated as my room. "Have you seen her?" I asked.

"Heard her," he said. "She's been moving around. Heard her tapping on the wall or something. At first, I thought it was you, but I came out here to find that no one else was around. I was lying in wait for her to show herself when you two came along."

I sensed more than saw Tony's puzzled frown. "The place is haunted," I explained.

"Oh," he said quietly. "I guess I should have guessed that. The inn is named after her?"

I nodded. "Years ago, she was famous for running down Kennedy Hill Road in her underwear in the middle of winter. I guess she got tired of being cold and decided to move in here." I turned to Mr. Rivers. "Is she still stealing stuff?"

"She grabbed all the change off my dresser!" I saw the dim shape before us shrug. "Granted, it was just twenty-six cents, but it's the principal of the thing! I can't have ghosts running around the inn, pilfering rings and change like she owns the place!"

~ 47 ~

I wasn't sure if owners should pilfer either, but I wanted to get past Mr. Rivers and into my room so that Tony and I could get jiggy, so I refrained from pointing this out. "We'll keep an eye out for her if you like, sir."

"Don't leave any valuables lying around. That's my advice! She's in a mischievous mood!"

Mr. Rivers seemed to want to stick around in the hall, which was his prerogative, but if he heard some moans and groans coming from inside my room, that was his own fault. I reached out and grasped the doorknob. "Well, we'll be careful," I said as we slid by Rivers and into the room.

While it was "my" room, I had actually only been in it a few times, so turning on the lights would have been a good idea, but Tony and I hadn't been together—naked, anyway—in such a long time that little things, like being able to see what the hell I was doing, weren't exactly a priority. I closed the door behind us, and we made it two paces inside before we were kissing and fondling and pulling at clothes.

It's an odd thing about clothes—you don't really give them much thought when they're on you. Oh, I know some people fret about what to wear each day, but once they've got the garments on they generally don't continue fretting. They just go about their day, being clothed. Personally, I've always favored T-shirts and jeans. Easy on, easy off. Comfortable and practical. Somehow, though, when you've got someone with you that you want to get naked with, clothes decide to be contrary. "Yeah, you're not getting me off that easy," your T-shirt will say, and before you know it, the thing's all over your face and one sleeve is hooked on your elbow and you have to twist around like Houdini getting out of a straightjacket. That button on your jeans, which normally is easy to undo, suddenly won't budge, no matter how hard you tug at the damned thing. This also happens when you have to pee so bad it hurts, but that's another story. And untying your shoes? Forget it. Kick the suckers off. That's the only way. In kicking off my right shoe, I may have flipped it and it may have hit a lamp and the lamp may have been knocked off the table and there may have been the sound of breaking glass, but I wasn't sure. I was too busy trying to kiss Tony with my T-shirt half on my face, covering my eyes and refusing to relinquish its death grip.

The blinds were up on the window, so there was a little light coming in, although not much. My room faced the backyard, and there was a large tree, currently leafless and a little spooky looking, close enough to my window that its branch snaked out and touched the pane. The wind caused this branch, which looked somewhat like a skeletal hand, to scrape across the glass. The shadow it cast on the wall looked like something out of a horror movie. I ignored the tree. I had other things to think about.

Tony managed to get his shirt off and his pants down to his ankles. I scored a victory over my T-shirt and flung it aside. A lot of fondling and rubbing and moaning ensued. We had to get to the bed or I was going to burst. I broke off our kiss and concentrated on undoing my pants. With a little hard work I got them unbuttoned, unzipped, and down. I kicked my way out of them, nearly losing my balance and falling against Tony, who laughed and kissed me.

"We'd better get to the bed," he whispered.

"Yes, I think that's a good idea."

We started to move toward the dark shape against the wall, which I knew from my earlier reconnaissance was the bed. I held Tony's hand as we went, reveling in the inner spark I got from just touching him. I may have been a little excited and moved too fast in a dark, unfamiliar room, as I collided with something hard.

"Ouch. Careful," I warned. "There's a chair there."

The last few steps to the bed were done with awkward hops as the rest of our clothes came off. Socks were flung to the shadows. I think my underwear caught on one of the blades of the ceiling fan. The important thing is that by the time we sank onto the mattress, we were naked as jaybirds, a phrase I'd picked up from my father when he was still around. An odd phrase, as jaybirds are covered in feathers. If you saw a naked jaybird, sans feathers, I'm thinking you'd have to point and laugh. Rude, but how could you help yourself?

"I've been looking forward to this," Tony said. His voice was husky.

I'm sure mine was too. "Worth missing my meatloaf dinner for?"

He pretended to have to ponder that. "Maybe," he said with a smile.

It seemed my heart was pounding in my ears. Somehow, getting naked in a fairly unfamiliar room seemed to amp up the excitement level, like we were doing something we shouldn't. And—praise Madonna!—we were going to beat the Boyfriend Zone! My nether regions were shouting, telling me we'd had enough of small talk and needed to get down to business. To appease them, I kissed Tony, and we rolled around until I was on top of him. Our hands were roaming everywhere, and things were getting to the point of no return when he suddenly stopped.

"Shit!" he exclaimed. "Do we have condoms and lube?"

Like the Boy Scouts, I always come prepared. "In my jeans," I said. Reluctantly, I got off Tony and scrambled to the side of the bed. With my legs precariously perched on the mattress, I leaned out as far as I could and started searching around on the floor. I had to brace myself with my right hand while my left did the hunting. The room wasn't that big, and I couldn't believe that my jeans, although hastily discarded, weren't within grabbing distance. I leaned out more, straining the muscles. I found one of Tony's socks. Close but no cigar. A shoe. Pants! No, they were Tony's. Where the hell were mine?

I looked up at the window, wondering why the moon couldn't be more accommodating and provide just a bit more illumination, and saw a face. Outside, hovering just out the bedroom window, was a nasty, evil-looking face. I just got a fleeting glimpse, but I registered fierce, mean eyes blazing with hatred. Surprised by seeing a face just hanging around outside a third-floor window, I lost my balance and fell out of the bed.

Rat Bastard

My left elbow took the brunt of the fall, and some cussing ensued as I cradled the injured limb and did a bit of rolling. I think the exact phrase that escaped my lips was shitdamnhellblastmotherfucker, but I may have left out a syllable or two. I attempt to keep my cursing to a minimum, as I had an aunt who found it distasteful, and I'd promised her I'd avoid profanity if at all possible, but this was one of those just-not-possible times. I was still getting pains shooting through the left appendage when Tony hopped out of bed and came to my side. "Weasel, are you all right?"

"The face!"

"You fell on your face?"

"No, at the window!" I stopped rolling. The pain had subsided. I flapped the wing around a little to ensure nothing was broken. No, it had just been a jar to the inaptly named funny bone. I was going to live. I was still reeling, though, from the sight that had caused the spill from the bed. I glanced at the window.

The face was gone.

Chapter Six

I DON'T know about you. Maybe there are some people who, getting ready for some bouncy-bouncy on the bed only to spot a head floating outside a third-floor window just as things are getting going, can just shrug it off and say, "Nice trick. Now, where were we?" and go back to the Horizontal Hokey Pokey. I'm not one of those people. For one, my heart was doing an imitation of Usain Bolt, and my brain was asking, "What? What was that? What's going on? I want some answers here!" So, minutes later, rather than running my hands across Tony's luscious skin, I was outside with him, our clothes hastily put back on, armed with flashlights, searching for scary faces. Hopefully attached to a body. I knew the joint was supposed to be haunted, but seriously, don't, if you're a ghost, just show up as a floating face. Give us the whole body. Bad enough seeing something that's not supposed to be there, but when you throw in floating body parts, well, that's just going too far.

The logical part of my brain told me this face wasn't a ghost. It must have been someone in the tree outside my room, although why they had a face that looked like something Doc Frankenstein put together hastily and then discarded is beyond me. I wasn't sure which choice I was hoping for, human or ghost.

It was pretty cold out, and Tony was still trying to zip up his coat as we rounded the corner of the house and headed toward the tree outside my window. We stopped as he struggled with the zipper, his flashlight cradled in his armpit. "Okay, got it," he announced. We only went another step before he stopped again. "Wait. Did something fall out of my pocket?"

I played my beam over the grass around his feet. "Don't see anything."

"I thought I heard something drop. Guess it was nothing." We moved on, both of our beams shining on the tree looming out of the darkness before us. "You're sure it was a face."

"Eyes. Ears. Mouth. Nose. Can't get much more face than that."

"So it was either a ghost or someone in the tree."

"Or someone on a long ladder." We'd made it to the tree, and for some reason I reached out and touched the bark, like it was going to tell me if someone had recently climbed up it. It told me nothing. Sherlock Holmes would have just examined the tree through his lens and said, "Ah, Watson! I perceive that a man barely short of six feet has recently been up this oak, and furthermore, he was wearing size ten boots!" The big show-off. I didn't have a magnifying lens with me, and even if I did, it would only tell me that the tree was, indeed, made of wood. I shone my light up. It looked like there was a fairly big branch close to my window, one that just might support someone's weight. I then checked the ground at the base of the tree. "From the rain earlier, you'd think the ground would show footprints. But I can't see any." My favorite fictional detective would have thrown himself on the ground and checked to see if there were bent or broken blades of grass and deduced from that how tall the mysterious man was, and no doubt could have informed Watson they were looking for a baker with a slight limp, a wife who no longer loved him, and who owned a spaniel with bad teeth. It was too freaking cold for me to sprawl across the ground and get stains on my jacket, and I'm sure the only deduction I would have come up with anyway was that it was dark outside and I couldn't see much even with the flashlight, certainly not footprints or broken blades of grass or any other sign of the baker with the limp. If he existed.

I don't know what I expected to find. Maybe some dude shinnying down the tree, or at least a fleeting glimpse of him darting around the side of the house, but there was no sign anyone had been out there. I looked at Tony. His coat was heavier than mine, and he was shivering. "What do you think?" I asked.

"I think I need a drink. I'm freezing my balls off!"

I made a sour face, which was pointless, as his flashlight wasn't pointed my way, so my facial features probably weren't too clear. "You're right. Whoever the guy was, he's long gone." I sighed as we began to retrace our footsteps. "Let's go to Rockford. It's not too late. We can hit the Twenty-One Club."

"You sure?" There was a hint of disappointment in his voice, and I knew he was hoping we'd just get some alcohol from the Phantom Lady's bar and head back to my room, but the truth was, I wasn't sure I wanted to do that. Sure, I wanted to have sex with Tony and quell the specter looming over us that was the Boyfriend Zone, but that room was tainted now in my mind. I'd be enjoying the humping—because who wouldn't with Tony as a partner—but part of me would be wondering if I happened to glance around if I'd see the evil face again. And that kind of thing puts you off lovemaking.

"I'm sure. Then we can head to my apartment in town. Just have to make sure we make it back here for my shift tomorrow."

Tony chuckled. "It's odd, hearing you talk about work."

"It is, isn't it?" I put my arm around him as we walked. "Come on. I'll drive. We'll be there in no time."

As it turned out, we should have stayed at the Phantom Lady, even with weird, frightening faces appearing in windows.

THE TRIP to Rockford was fun. Number of Phantom Ladies spotted en route: zero. But Tony and I chatted and laughed, and by the time we pulled off the highway, I had almost—almost—forgotten about the face at the window. We made pretty good time, and before long we were in downtown Rockford, approaching one of the few gay bars in the area. The Twenty-One Club wasn't big. It wasn't flashy. But it was ours. The parking lot was across the street, and I was about to pull in when I saw Tony stiffen in his seat. He was staring out the window.

"What's going on?"

On the sidewalk, mostly huddled around the streetlamp, were about fifteen people, most of whom were carrying signs. They looked angry, determined, and very, very cold. I groaned.

"Protesters? Really? In December? Don't they have something better to do than picket a gay bar, like feed the homeless or something?"

They had had protesters outside the club on numerous occasions, and for the most part, they were just silly people who wanted to hand you a leaflet telling you how you could be saved from a life of sin if you attended their church. People from my stepfather's church had camped out there many a time, and it shows just how much the Incident of the Face at the Window had affected me that I didn't see the danger looming. Suffice it to say I was perfectly happy as Tony and I parked and got out of the car. It wasn't until we hit the sidewalk that I had a premonition of doom, and then it was too late. I didn't see the stepmonster at first, but his bellow made his presence known, not only to me but to people slumbering in nearby houses and anyone else in, and I may be exaggerating but not by much, a three-mile radius. It was a loud bellow.

"Patrick Carrington Weasley!"

I halted.

You've probably heard the story of Lot's wife. Famous story. I first learned of it at Mrs. Climthorpe's boarding school. Mrs. Climthorpe was fond of Bible stories, and the tale of Lot and his missus was one of her favorites. It goes something like this: God, being a little ticked off at the towns of Sodom and Gomorrah, decided to give them the old zap. As Lot was a pretty good guy, though, God warned him ahead of time. "If I were you," he said (I may be paraphrasing here—it's been a long time since I was at Mrs.

Climthorpe's), "I'd take a vacation. Leave town. Take the family. Go see the folks." So Lot packed up his things, and he and his family set off. God did have one codicil, though. "Oh, whatever you do, don't look back." History doesn't tell us Lot's reaction to this statement, but he most likely said, "Huh? Say what?" and God replied with a stern, "You heard me. There's going to be a lot of fire and brimstone and things going up in smoke and people screaming. So don't turn and look. I want to be perfectly clear on this point." So there's Lot and the fam, trudging away, while behind them there's death and destruction. Lot's wife (if Mrs. Climthorpe gave her name, I've forgotten it, so we'll just call her Margot) couldn't resist the temptation and looked back, which, you've got to admit, wasn't really smart. God's warning and all that. But here's the kicker. God turns old Margot into a pillar of salt. A pillar of salt! I mean, really! The birds and local animals were probably pretty pleased, but for Lot (and especially Margot) it was a pisser.

What I'm getting at here was that I froze just like Margot. Stopped midstride. Couldn't move. My blood seemed to freeze in my veins. Tony stopped too. Come to think of it, a lot of the protesters froze as well. It was that kind of a bellow from the stepmonster. Even those whose names weren't Patrick Carrington Weasley (which was all those present with the exception of me) stopped what they were doing and did a statue imitation. The only person moving was my stepmonster, and he was storming up through the throng to confront me.

"What," he asked when he was mere inches from my face, "are you doing here?" His face was purple with rage.

"Um," I said. I wanted to say more, but nothing came to me.

Dollings snarled at me, flashed an angry look at Tony by my side, and then returned to me. "I see that you have chosen not to abide by our agreement."

"I... I...." Ever notice how, when you really need it to kick into gear, your brain often checks out and stops functioning altogether? Stephen Hawking needs to look into this.

Rat Bastard

The stepmonster seemed to suddenly be aware that his cronies were still there within earshot, watching the scene intently. He lowered his voice so only Tony and I could hear him. "I told you I didn't want you to see this boy any longer."

"Excuse me, but—" Tony began.

Dollings stopped him with a glare. "I'm talking to my stepson, if you don't mind." To me, he said, "I want you to go home immediately. Not to your apartment, but to the house. I'll deal with you first thing in the morning."

I found my voice. Where it had been hiding up to this point, I don't know. It came out a little thin and reedy, but it was audible. "I can't."

The stepmonster's eyes flashed. "What?" he demanded.

"I can't. Or, more to the point, I won't." I was aware my knees were shaky and threatening to just give out and refuse to hold me up any longer, but I pressed on, my voice getting a little more forceful as it warmed up. "I came here with my boyfriend. We're going to go inside and have a drink. I believe I'm going to need a few, actually. I'll come and see you Monday morning, after my classes. I'm sure you'll take away my allowance, car, and everything else you can get your hands on. I'll give you the shirt off my back, if it'll make you happy. But for now, right now, I'm with Tony. And you're being rude to him, so we're going to leave now and get a drink and I'll see you Monday morning."

And I turned to go, hardly daring to breathe. There's another Bible story I learned at Mrs. Climthorpe's, this one about David and Goliath. I'm a little fuzzy on the details, but this Goliath guy was a mighty warrior (one of the Philistines, if memory serves), all decked out in armor. He challenges the Israelites to send out a champion to fight him. David, armed with only a sling and a couple of stones, accepts. Goliath sort of laughs at this, saying something like, "Yeah, really?" And David puts a stone in the sling and flings it and bonks Goliath right smack in the middle of the forehead. Down goes Goliath, and David cuts off his head. (That part I remember for sure, nice and gory.) Anyway, I wonder if David, on facing this big dude all in armor, was all sure of himself and brave, or if, like me standing up to the stepmonster, his knees shook like bric-a-brac during an earthquake.

"Are you okay, Weasel?" Tony asked. His voice sounded very far away.

"I need," I said, "alcohol. Big glass filled with alcohol. Maybe laced with strychnine."

I knew that life, as I knew it, was over. I felt an odd mixture of pride over standing up to the stepmonster and sheer terror at what lay ahead for me.

I DIDN'T feel any better in the morning. Once I'd forced the peepers open and convinced myself I wasn't dead, I sat up in bed and took stock. I was in my bed at the Phantom Lady Inn. I was wearing the clothes I'd had on the previous evening, although my shoes were off. Tony wasn't present, and thinking of him caused my heart to get that leaden feeling. I'd messed things up royally. What had started off as a fantastic date night had quickly deteriorated to the point where I wouldn't blame Tony if he called it quits. Well, okay, there had been a flaming cutting board and a scary face and a tumble out of bed, but that was fantastic compared to how the evening ended.

There was a note on the nightstand. I snatched it up in a quick motion I immediately regretted. My head was punishing me from an overabundance of gin and tonics, and I had the impression a marching band was currently pounding around my cranium, and the tune they were playing was something loud and insistent and more like something from the Sex Pistols than John Philip Sousa. To appease the noggin, I moved more slowly and put the note up to the optics. At first it seemed to be written in Sanskrit, but soon my eyes focused and I could make out the words.

> *Weas:*
> *You were pretty out of it last night by the time we*
> *left the club. I got your keys out of your pocket, as*

there was no way I was going to let you drive. You were barely coherent. Got you into bed the best I could. You kept saying something about shrimp screaming and you couldn't hear anything. Wish I could have stayed, but I have to be back at work. I'll call you later.

    Love,

    Tony.

It didn't sound like he was giving me the push, but I couldn't expect someone like Tony to break up with me via a note. He'd do the proper thing and break my heart in person. I took stock.

1. My stepfather would shortly be taking away my allowance and, I was sure, my car. This would leave me with no money and no transport. A bad thing.

2. My date with Tony had been an unmitigated disaster. I'd nearly set a kitchen on fire, and I ended up too drunk to even recall leaving the bar. A bad thing.

3. I was still wearing my clothes. Which meant Tony and I never got to finish having sex. I was sure this was a mark against me. He must be thinking, "This Weasel is a great guy, but we never seem to be able to get naked and have fun. Either he's seeing weird faces in windows or he's too drunk to stand up. I'd better break it off with him." A really, really bad thing.

OH, YEAH. And one of the local deputy sheriffs suspects I'm the local pyromaniac.

There didn't seem to be much reason to get out of bed, so I lay back down and tried to reconnect with Morpheus. My hangover seemed to have other ideas and decided to add the "Anvil Chorus" to the marching band. I tried to cover my head with a pillow, but that merely resulted in *muffled* bangs. I tried another pillow. That helped, but it was hard to breathe. I threw the pillows aside. Miraculously, there was a cessation of the thumps. It occurred to me the banging wasn't in my head after all, but was in fact coming from somewhere down the hall. I threw back the covers and got out of bed. It took two tries, but I managed it.

I padded out of my room and down the hall in my stocking feet. The banging recommenced, and now I recognized the sound as a nail being hit by a hammer. Frowning, I searched for the source of the cacophony.

Standing just inside his room on a ladder was Mr. Rivers. I could only see him from the chest down, but it was obviously he who was pounding nails. I poked my head into his room and saw he was engaged in rigging up some netting on the ceiling just inside his door. An odd decorative choice, I thought, but then I'm no Martha Stewart. He realized someone was present, and he looked down, taking a nail out of his mouth so he could speak.

"Ah, Wombat. You're up. I hope I didn't disturb you."

"No, not at all," I replied. You can't always be truthful. "Um… can I help in any way?"

"Almost finished, actually." Whatever it was he was working on, it looked complicated. There was a net and a lot of boards and levers and wires. He glanced at the nail he'd removed from his mouth. He must have decided it was a spare, because he proceeded to pound it into the ceiling some inches away from his contraption where it could serve no purpose whatsoever. "All I have to do is work my trip wire down, and eureka will be the word of the day."

I blinked. "Trip wire?"

"Yes. I'm setting a trap for our ghost." I must have looked confused, for he went on to explain. "When this is done, I'll have a cord running down the side of the door. This will be stretched across the doorway at night, so that anyone coming in will cause the netting to fall, effectively trapping themselves."

Rat Bastard

I had a lot of questions but chose just one. "Can ghosts get caught by nets?"

"Ah. Probably not." Rivers didn't seem worried about the logic of this. He started down the ladder. It was a nice, solid aluminum ladder that was sturdy as hell, but he still wobbled a bit coming down, so I held it firmly as he descended. I even took him by the elbow to make sure he was safely on the ground. I was never a Boy Scout, but I knew my stuff, and making sure older guys didn't plummet off ladders was all part of the Weasel way of life. "But," he said, looking thankful to be on solid ground, "if the trap is sprung and there's nothing there, then I've succeeded, haven't I? I'll know the Phantom Lady has been in my room without doubt."

"It looks impressive," I said. It didn't really, but he was my boss.

"Yes, it is, isn't it?" He was beaming with pride. "The culprit, you see, only has to walk over the threshold and—whoosh!—he's caught! The net falls on him—or in this case, her—and then we've got them!"

Again, I wondered about the logic. If ghosts can walk through walls, surely they would go right through a trip wire if they so desired. Moreover, the contraption looked like it wouldn't work at all, or if it did it would bring half the ceiling down along with the net. I refrained from pointing this out, but Mr. Rivers seemed to read my mind.

"The trap serves two purposes, you see." He chuckled as he brushed some ceiling plaster off his hands. "If the trap is sprung and the net falls on no one, then we know our petty thief—who, by the way, made off with my St. Christopher medal—is not of this world, but the next. However, there's always the chance the thief is flesh and blood. If that's the case, he'll have a lot of explaining to do. Either way, we'll have our answer."

"Brilliant," I said, although loony was probably more to the point.

He gazed up at his handiwork. "Yes, I believe it is. I don't suppose, Weasel my boy, that you'd volunteer to test it for me? Give me a few minutes to set the trip wire, and come in, and—"

"I wish I had the time, but I've got to get going. Things to do, people to see. You know how it is."

"Some other time, then?"

"Sure. Oh, and I'm sorry about setting that cutting board on fire last night. Knock it off my wages, of course."

"Oh, it was just a cutting board. I'm sure I've set dozens of them aflame in my time. Think nothing of it."

"If you're sure. My bad luck that Deputy Bradley was standing outside. Now he's really suspicious of me."

"That was my fault. His being here, I mean. I called him. Saw someone lurking outside, acting very shifty."

A chill filled my heart. "I saw a face last night, in my window!"

"Really?"

"Not a nice face. I really didn't get the details, but whoever it was didn't look happy."

"So we either have ghosts," Rivers said, "or prowlers. Or both."

I glanced up at his trap. Maybe it wasn't such a daft idea after all.

MONDAY AFTER my classes, I showed up at Chez Weasley to receive punishment. Walking down the hall to my stepmonster's den was like walking the last mile. When I was finally ushered into his sanctum, I expected him to be livid and that loads of shouting and recriminations would ensue, but he was sitting behind his desk, quietly smoldering.

"Sit," he told me.

I did so.

He held out his palm. "Keys."

I was expecting that. With a sigh, I fished out the keys to the Corvette and handed them over. He put them away in the top drawer.

"I don't have to tell you," he said evenly, "that you're cut off from here on out."

I sighed. "I'm not going to stop seeing Tony."

I hadn't been able to see Tony since the date from hell, but we'd spoken on the phone, and I was shocked to learn he wasn't going to dump me. Actually, he was the one who called me. He'd called from the phone in the kitchen in Winston Manor, as he'd misplaced his cell phone. At first, I thought he was only calling to see if he'd left it with me, and my replies were glum to say the least until he goaded me into confessing that I thought he was ending things between us. "I understand," he'd said. "I'd have gotten shit-faced if all that had happened to me. There will be other nights."

There would? If Tony was such a wonderful guy that he'd overlook the date from hell, then there was no way I could let him down by agreeing to any scheme Dollings proposed. I wasn't even going to lie about it. Tony and I were an item… or at least I hoped we were becoming one. Dollings could cut me off without a cent, take away my car, whatever. I'd be poor and starving and have tired feet, but I'd have Tony. So be it.

That didn't change the fact that, sitting across from the stepmonster, I felt that my life was over. I wasn't exactly hearing Chopin's Funeral March in my head, but the musicians were tuning up. Not that he (Chopin) called it the Funeral March. I think he just said it was his Piano Sonata No. 2 in B-flat minor or some such thing. If he'd gone to his friends and said, "Hey, guys! I've just written this thing. I call it the Funeral March," they'd probably have said, "Whoa, dude! That sounds like a bummer! I'd rename it if you want it to get any airplay."

I was thinking of a snappy comeback by Chopin to his friends, maybe something along the lines that the radio hadn't been invented yet so they shouldn't be using words like airplay if they didn't want to look like total asses, when my stepmonster spoke. "Go on seeing him if you want. It will, of course, mean that you'll be getting absolutely no money from here on out."

"Except for school, naturally."

Dollings cocked an eyebrow. "No money whatsoever. You can pay for college on your own."

If it's possible to crumble while you're sitting down, I crumbled. I felt like all my bones had just vacated and I was reduced to jelly. The prospect of being *totally* cut off hadn't even occurred to me. My mind raced. Tuition for next semester had already been paid, so I was safe there. I'd just have to put in many hours at the inn to pay for next year or get a student loan. That scene played through my mind.

"Hi. My name is Weasel. I'd like for you to give me money so that I can keep going to college."

Student loan guy: "Of course. Wait a minute! Don't you come from a family that has money by the truckload?"

"Yes, but they won't give me any because I'm gay and they're homophobes."

Student loan guy: "Sounds like a personal problem to me. Why don't you please the homophobes and marry Cicely Talbot and see Tony on the sly?"

Mentally, I kicked the student loan guy in the nads. That made me feel slightly better.

"I suppose," I said to the stepmonster, speaking softly, "this makes you very happy." I was speaking softly, but, unlike T. Roosevelt, I wasn't carrying a big stick, because if I had been, I'd have bonked him on the head with it.

Dollings didn't directly answer my question, but he smiled. "This doesn't bring me any personal enjoyment," he said. Liar. He shook his head in mock sadness. "If you'd only agree to a few requests of mine—"

"Like not seeing my boyfriend and going out with a loon."

"Cicely Talbot isn't a loon."

"She'll do until a better loon comes along. Tell me, why does my going out with Tony get your undies in a twist so much? It's not like it has anything to do with you. I know your church is all 'gay is evil' and 'they want to turn our children gay' and other such idiocies, but I'm not even your kid! I'm a stepson! You can shake your head in church and tell your buddies that you've got a burdensome cross to bear, so to speak, and they'll pat you on the back and offer to buy you a stiff whiskey and soda to help you to forget that you've got a spawn of Satan in your midst."

The smile was replaced by an arched eyebrow. Whatever else you want to say about Jasper K. Dollings, his face is one animated piece of flesh. "You want me to tell you why I despise you so much, is that what you want?"

"Might as well get it out in the open." I was a little surprised at myself. Normally I avoid confrontation. There might be a little French blood in me. When someone wants to argue, some part of me just wants to sip wine, eat something swimming in a rich sauce, say "Oui" a lot, and just get the whole thing over with so I can go take a nap or something. Especially if, as in the present case, the other person in the discussion is undoubtedly possessed by a particularly nasty demon. A demon with irritable bowel syndrome.

But here's the thing about the French (and me): they can only be pushed so far before they square their shoulders and they scream "That's enough!" and you end up with a bayonet in your gizzard. Like Claude Rains in *Casablanca.* He goes through the whole movie saying, "Nope. Don't want to get involved. Not my business. I don't care." But by the end, the Germans have irritated him so much that he walks off into the fog holding hands with Humphrey Bogart. (At least that's how I remember it.) Granted, Claude Rains was really English and just playing some French dude, but you get my point.

To be honest, though, sitting across from the stepmonster, I may have appeared to be brave, but inwardly I was shaking. If, and since we're talking about Jasper Dollings here this was a distinct possibility, he suddenly sprouted horns and began breathing fire, I'd have been out of my chair in a flash, running and screaming like a girl in one of those old black-and-white mummy movies. (Note: how did the Mummy ever catch anyone? He trudged along at a snail's pace but yet always caught up with his victim, who suddenly found themselves unable to walk two feet without tripping over something.

The Mummy must have had his lucky rabbit's foot handy, is all I'm saying.)

"Are you even listening to me?" the stepmonster bellowed.

I hadn't been, of course. I knew I'd asked a question, but then the mind was busy with French Claude Rainses and demons and Lon Chaney wrapped in bandages. "Sorry," I admitted, "I was thinking about the Mummy."

"Well, you can forget about running to your mother and trying to convince her to give you your allowance back. She's with me on this." Dollings leaned forward, pointing a finger at me. "I don't like you."

"I had noticed." I thought about telling him I'd been referring to *the* Mummy, the dude all wrapped in bandages in the old Universal monster movies and not *my* mummy, but I let it drop.

"I don't like your lifestyle. I don't like you flaunting your debauched way of thinking all over town."

"But I don't even live in this house anymore. Really, under normal circumstances, we need hardly ever meet. I have my apartment and school and you have your business. I can just pop in at Thanksgiving and Christmas and wave a tentacle and be off on my merry way. Minimal contact."

The stepmonster wasn't listening. "You and your kind are an abomination. The Bible clearly states—"

"That you shouldn't eat shellfish or have a tattoo. If I recall correctly, you love lobster and have an anchor tattooed on your right arm."

Dollings sputtered. "What?"

"Leviticus 11:10. Can't eat things in the water unless they have fins and scales. Leviticus also says you can't eat camel, badger, and a lot of other stuff, which, I have to say, I'm with them one hundred percent there. And I think it's Leviticus chapter nineteen or thereabouts that says you can't have a tattoo. Got a Bible handy? I can find it pretty fast, if you want the exact wording."

Rat Bastard

The veins in the stepmonster's neck were standing out and pulsing angrily. In fact, I was worried that he was set to explode, and then what? What if all the bits of exploded Dollings then grew into individual Dollings? We'd have hundreds of stepmonsters running about. Not good. His face twitched more than William Shatner's did when he was yelling, "Khan!" in *Star Trek II.* "Get out!" he thundered.

"Can't," I said.

He Shatnered even more. "What?"

"Can't. You took my car. The buses don't come out this far. I sure as heck ain't walking. I'd blow out my tennis shoes. So, I guess I'll be staying here. It'll give us a chance to bond. Dinners together, and every evening we can play Monopoly. I have to be the top hat, though. Top hats are cool."

I was taking a chance. I was trying to make him mad enough to cave a little, but there was always the possibility I'd push too hard and he'd fly across the desk and throttle me. And, for just a second, I think that was the choice he was going for, but then he slid my keys across the desk toward me. "Just go," he growled. "Get out of here. We'll discuss your transportation options later."

I snapped up the keys and hightailed it out of his den as fast as my legs would take me.

Score: Middle-aged homophobic douche bag with scraggly mustache—zero. Tall, blond, marvelously sexy college student nicknamed after a member of the family Mustelidae—one.

Chapter Seven

I WAS having a pretty good Tuesday, as Tuesdays go. I'd taken two finals—one in history and one in my folklore class—and I felt confident about both of them. A light snow was falling, and I was hopeful of a white Christmas. I'm not sure why I was wanting this, as I'd never had a pleasant, Danny Kaye singing his heart out, Bing Crosby, Currier-and-Ives-type Christmas in my life, but maybe this one would be different. I had a boyfriend, even if we were having trouble with that pesky Boyfriend Zone, and I had a job. True, other than the dough I was getting from Mr. Rivers for standing around doing basically nothing, I was broke, but what the hey. Life could be worse. I could be on a reality TV show. Or worse, on *Maury*. "Is Weasel the father of your son? Let's find out!"

Um… not very likely, Maury. Sorry.

I was heading to where I'd parked my car (which, despite my stepfather's threats, was still in my possession) when my cell phone sprang to life, chirping for all it was worth. I fished it out and saw I had a text message from Tony. I frowned as I read it.

Emergency. Meet me Alpine Park 6:30 tonight.

Those who know me know I love mysteries, but this message seemed to be greatly lacking in detail. Emergency. What kind of emergency? And what kind of emergency can wait until six thirty? The very word emergency evokes a feeling of urgency, not of waiting around, thumbs a-twiddling, until the sun has long since set. And why a meeting in a park? Nice, though, that Tony had located his cell phone. Last I'd heard, he still couldn't find it. I sent a text back.

Confused. What emergency? Can meet you now, as I'm done with school for the day. Need me to come out to see you?

I had arrived at my car by this point and was just settling into the driver's seat when I got a reply.

Wait until 6:30 at Alpine Park. See you then.

I inserted the key into the ignition but waited until I'd tapped out a reply before starting the engine.

Worried. What emergency? Call me, or I can call you. Texting is stupid under circumstances. Dialing in 6.4 seconds.

I hadn't even backed the car out of the space when another text arrived.

No! Don't call! Can't explain now. Just meet me 6:30 Alpine Park. Very important.

I hit more keys.

Emergency or just very important? Huge difference.

Figuring the answer would come quickly, I sat with the motor idling. I didn't want to pull into traffic and have to send another text. I didn't have long to wait.

Just be there!!!! Stop being annoying and just meet me!!!!

That made my frown deepen. It wasn't like Tony to call me annoying. What with our schedules and living in different towns, we often went mad with texts or had marathon phone conversations. Tony knew how I hated to be serious, and I was surprised by his reaction. It must, I concluded, be something particularly unpleasant he had to tell me, but I still couldn't figure out why I had to wait and go to a park to discover what it was. I was admittedly new to this having a boyfriend thing, so maybe I didn't understand all the rules. Realizing I'd crossed a line, I typed back a simple reply.

Just trying to make you smile. Will be there, of course. Love you.

I waited for a minute, expected another text. When none came, I set the phone on the passenger seat and proceeded on. At the first stoplight I came to, I checked the phone, thinking perhaps I had missed the signal telling me another text had been received. No texts, but I did notice my battery was nearly depleted, so much so that it was only a short jag down the street before the phone gave out that little chirp that meant "Hey, dummy! Plug me in or I'm going dead!"

Biting my lip, I did some quick thinking. The phone would be dead by the time I got to my apartment, and what if, in the meantime, Tony sent me an update, perhaps changing the venue or time? I'd be out in the park, freezing my katootie off, and no Tony in sight. It would be quicker to stop by my mom's place and grab a charger there. It would be safe, as the Dreaded Dollings would still be at work, and I would get a chance to confront Mom on her own and maybe get her to relent a little on the allowance situation. Kill two birds, as they say, with one stone. I changed course slightly and navigated toward the homestead.

I was a block away from home when the car engine made a funny sort of sound. It suddenly went into a high-pitched squeal for a second or two before settling back down and behaving normally. Hearing the sound, my heart gave a little lurch, accompanied by every nerve in my body saying, "Oh, this isn't good." Fortunately, after this little hiccup the motor seemed fine, and I proceeded merrily along.

Mom wasn't home, or so I was informed by Rita, having gone into town for art supplies. Ma had, it seemed, signed up for an artist's retreat and had packed her easel and paints and brushes into one of the stepmonster's several cars in preparation for a wonderful weekend painting trees and possibly nude bodies. Rita, taking advantage of having the house to herself, was treating herself to a cup of coffee and a big slice of cake, feeling that (and quite rightly too, in my opinion) since her employers thought she didn't work much anyway, she might as well oblige them by putting her feet up and enjoying life while still on the clock. I joined her, and we jawed for a bit, enjoying some laughs about the old days. I was lost in the conversation, and it wasn't until Rita noticed the room was getting fairly dark that I realized it was later than I'd thought.

The clock on the wall had both hands dangerously close to the six and twelve, little and big respectively, which meant I was in danger of not only missing my appointment with Tony but could, if I didn't hoof it quickly, end up meeting Dollings on his way home from work. My phone was charged to the max by this time, so I kissed Rita on the cheek, causing a major blush, and hoofed it back out to the car. I threw myself in and turned the key.

Nothing.

Figuring I just hadn't given it enough of a twist, I tried again. This time the engine gave a sort of cough and a sputter before emitting that groan which is a car's way of saying "Oh, fuck it, I'm done."

"I don't have time for this," I told the vehicle and pumped the gas pedal before turning the key again. I'm not quite sure why people do this, as in my experience it doesn't ever do anything except give your right foot a little workout. The engine coughed again and then did a Marcel Marceau impression. "No!" I yelled. And then I slammed my hands hard against the steering wheel, so I had sore hands *and* a car that wouldn't run.

I thought. The thinking went fast, and the conclusion was really a no-brainer. I mean, I was sitting in a drive, looking at a four-car garage, and I knew at least two of those spaces were occupied by perfectly drivable cars and the keys to said cars would be on a hook just inside the back door. Technically, yes, the cars weren't mine, but it was the Weasley homestead, and I was a Weasley, and I felt, under the circumstances, that I was entitled to borrow one of them. If the clock wasn't against me, I might have pondered this a little more and come up with other solutions, but time had thrown down the gauntlet and basically was taunting me, calling me a chicken. "I'm a-wasting," it was saying, "and you're a putz if you don't act now." Accordingly, I was out of my Corvette in a flash and was hightailing it back indoors. I didn't even look to see which key I grabbed. Any working vehicle would do. Rita, alerted to my return by the hurried slamming of doors and the tromp of my feet through the house, came to see what was up.

I gave her another kiss on the cheek. "Gotta grab one of the stepmonster's cars. Don't tell him. I should have it back before he notices that it's gone." Without waiting for her reply, which would have been, knowing her, some warning I was courting death, I darted out to the garage.

The keys I grabbed belonged to my stepfather's new diamond-white metallic Mercedes-Benz coupe. It was a sweet looking ride, and I think I felt a tiny twinge of guilt as I gunned the engine and pulled out of the garage, knowing it cost more than 150,000 smackers and had been coddled by its owner since they had set eyes on each other in the showroom. I doubt if Dollings had ever pushed the engine into doing more than fifty miles per hour. I think I was doing that as I spun out of the driveway onto the road.

There was some rustling in the backseat as I took the corner, and I glanced back to see what was shifting about. It was my mom's painting stuff, and I saw that she had indeed shoved nearly everything she could back there. Not only were there canvases and paints, but she'd also covered most of her paraphernalia with her dirty paint rags. I could tell they were used by the odor of turpentine that assailed my nostrils. My guilt fled. Anyone who defiled the backseat of a lovely car like the Mercedes-Benz CL63 AMG Coupe with grimy rags deserved to have it borrowed by the son of the household for an emergency. Rationalization can be a wonderful thing.

Since we were close to the winter solstice, it was dark by the time I arrived at the park. The parks in Rockford close at dusk, and again I wondered why Tony chose that spot for our meeting. I parked the Merc on the street just outside the park and got out. It was damned cold, and dark clouds covered the moon and stars, but there was enough light from the houses nearby that I could navigate through the park without killing myself. I zipped up my hoodie and wished I'd worn something warmer. Shivering, I walked along a dirt path, passing trees and not much else, scanning the area for any sign of Tony. One would think he'd have been right at the park's entrance, making finding him easy. Not so. I pressed on.

Ahead, I spotted a dark figure leaning against a tree. I picked up my pace, but then slowed as I got a better gander at the person. He was a mere shadow, a dark shape next to another dark shape that had dark, barren shapes in the form of branches hanging down from it. Oddly, though, the dark shape that was supposed to be Tony didn't match up. Too big, for one thing. Tony was certainly easy on the eyes, but even his most ardent admirers, of whom I was president, wouldn't go so far as to say he was overly muscular. Thinnish, to be truthful. The shape before me seemed bulkier. And there was a glow of red up near his face, telling me this guy was smoking a cigarette. Tony was a nonsmoker. I still approached, but now with some trepidation and caution. Even if, as it was plainly obvious, this particular shadow wasn't Tony, the apple of my eye was still in the park somewhere, and I'd have to get past this ominous-looking shape to find him.

I went for the nonchalant attitude, with my hands in my pockets, just a guy out walking in a park after dark. I would nod at the guy in passing and hope he wouldn't mug me. Not that he'd get much for his troubles other than a few coins, a nearly empty container of Tic Tacs, and a set of keys to a Mercedes-Benz I didn't own.

The cigarette glowed as the guy took in a deep lungful. I was close enough to make out more details, but only that the dude had eyes, ears, a nose, and a mouth, a fact I had already assumed. A hand came up and took the ciggy from his mouth.

"Hey," he said. The voice was gruff.

"Hey," I replied, picking up my pace. I wanted to get past this smoker and find Tony. Getting closer, I could now see, with some help from a distant streetlamp, more of his face. And what I saw chilled my bones even more than the night air.

It was Gates Stumpenhorst. The very same Stumpenhorst who had once dated Tony and had accosted us outside McDonald's. The same Stumpenhorst who had threatened to, when next we met, beat the crap out of me and leave me twitching on the ground.

"So," he said, placing the cigarette back into his mouth and talking around it, "you're the little shit that wants to steal my Tony from me."

There were lots of things wrong with this sentence he spoke. First, I'm hardly a little shit. At six feet one, I was hardly little. Now, if he'd called me a skinny shit, I'd have objected to the noun but couldn't really have faulted him for the adjective. There wasn't a lot of meat on my bones. And I could have pointed out to him that I hadn't stolen Tony from him, as Tony had already dumped him before I came onto the scene. I could have pointed that out, but I didn't, because I was running away.

You might think that this was a chickenshit thing to do, and you'd be right. You know why the world is full of chickenshits? Because they have a survival instinct. We know when it's prudent to run away as fast as we can and when to stand and face the music. You've seen those guys in war movies, the ones sitting in some trench in France during WWII. There's always one who cockily says the enemy is far away and everything is safe. Then he sticks his head up over the trench and wham! Gets a bullet right between the eyes. I'm not that guy. I'm the guy who, moments previously, said to the cocky dude, "Yeah. Seems pretty quiet. Why don't you stick your head up and check to see if everything's all clear?"

I heard sounds behind me, so I knew Gates was in hot pursuit. I'm a good runner. Goodness knows I've had a lot of practice. I've run from the cops, friends wielding pointed sticks, angry dogs, and even one-night stands that turned out to be loopy on paint fumes. Under normal circumstances, I would have been confident I could outdistance the fit-but-heavier Stumpenhorst with no problem. Sort of like if the Incredible Hulk got ticked off at the Amazing Spider-Man. Sure, if he caught up with the lithe and limber wall-crawler, the Hulk would bash his brains in. But that's the trick, of course, getting Spider-Man to sit still long enough for you to smash your fist into his face. And while my version of the Hulk hadn't turned green and morphed into a huge CGI monster, I still didn't want to meet his knuckles up close. However, I was in an unfamiliar park after dark. At any moment, I could trip over a rock or the carcass of a squirrel or something. So when a tree with a convenient, low-hanging branch that looked like it would hold my weight presented itself, I took advantage of the situation and scrambled up.

Even this wasn't easy. The branch was still a good ways above my head, so I had to do a quick leap and a scramble, but after a few grunts and a rip in the knee of my jeans I managed it. I heard Stumpenhorst mutter an oath or two, and out of the corner of my eye I spotted him trying to leap up to grab hold of my branch. He missed on his first attempt, but, not wanting to take chances, I proceeded to monkey up the tree a little more, ending up nestled as close to the top as I could navigate. The branch I ended up on creaked under my weight, but it held. I looked down. Stumpenhorst was still trying to hoist himself up onto the lowest branch. He'd leap and grab hold, but when he tried to climb up he met with failure. The man had muscles and strength, of that I had no doubt, but he lacked my limberness. The cigarette was still clenched between his teeth. I could see the red glow brighten as he sucked in smoke. Apparently he'd missed the lecture telling people that not only was smoking bad for you, but it made you lose stamina when trying to do things like hoist yourself into a tree.

"Come down from there!" he yelled.

"I'm fine here, thank you very much," I said.

"When I get my hands on you, I'm going to throttle you!"

"You should work on your sales pitch," I replied. "If you're trying to entice me to come down, you're going about it all wrong."

I saw him leap up and grab hold of the branch again, with the same results. When he'd dropped back down to the ground, he glared up at me. "You're a dead man!"

I probably should have kept my trap shut. My voice seemed only to egg him on, but I felt the need to verbalize. When I was talking, I could, for a moment, forget that I was perched in a tree on a creaking branch with a madman waiting under me. "Philosophically speaking, we're all dying," I said. "I believe it was 1960s folk icon Bob Dylan who said, 'He not busy being born is busy dying.' In my philosophy class we were talking about—"

"Shut the hell up and come down here so I can bust your stupid face in!"

I didn't have a great view of my foe, as there was a good amount of darkness and barren branches between us, but I could tell he was wearing a fairly big coat. It might have even been something hunters used, as I thought I could see a camouflage pattern to it. It looked warm. I was in my hoodie, and my teeth were beginning to chatter. Still, what was a little chill compared to having your teeth bashed in? "I'm good here," I reiterated.

Stumpenhorst began pacing back and forth beneath me, reminding me of a tiger I'd seen at a zoo years ago. I'd have chosen the tiger over Stumpenhorst as a cellmate any day. As he did his to-and-fro, he'd look up at me every now and then. I couldn't really make out his eyes, but I'm sure they were not gazing at me with affection.

He was, I could see, stumped. A stumped Stumpenhorst! Sorry. He wanted to pound me to oblivion, but the lack of Weasel within hands' reach flummoxed him. An idea seemed to come to him, and he took a running jump at the branch. This time he got a better hold of it and managed to swing his feet over until they found purchase against the trunk of the tree. He hung there for a moment, and it was an even-money bet whether he'd be able to pull himself up or fall and hopefully break his stupid arm. Unfortunately for me, it was the former. He groaned and cursed and huffed and puffed, not unlike the wolf in that old tale involving a trio of pigs, but he made it. Once he'd secured a spot on that lowest branch, he glared up at me, an evil grin spreading across his face. Stumpenhorst didn't have a mustache, but if he had, I'm sure he would have done a Simon Legree twirl of it. He may have even uttered a triumphant "Aha!" but I can't be sure because I wasted no time myself and was playing Tarzan, leaping and climbing down branches, trying to keep on the opposite side of the tree from him. Adrenaline is a marvelous thing.

Rat Bastard

It would have been nice to have been able to pause and see the shock on his face, or even to hear him say, "Curses! Foiled again!" but I couldn't take the chance. I took a shortcut to the ground and skipped the last branch or two and just, quite literally, took a leap of faith. The impact was jarring and made my teeth clink together, but I didn't feel any bones snapping, so I righted myself as fast as I could and ran.

Behind me I heard "Shit" followed by "That little fucker" and the sound of Gates Stumpenhorst dropping out of the tree. I gathered from the string of epithets that came out of his mouth that his landing hadn't been as graceful as mine, but apparently he wasn't damaged beyond repair because seconds later I heard his rapid footsteps in hot pursuit of moi. Luckily, I had quite a head start on him, so, while I didn't dawdle, I wasn't overly worried either. The entrance to the park was just ahead of me, and now there was enough light from the street to ensure I could stay on the path and not trip over a chipmunk who had come out to see what all the commotion was about.

As I hit the sidewalk just outside the park, I flashed a backward glance. Stumpenhorst was in good shape, I'll give him that, and was quite a runner for a guy his size. I did note that the cigarette was still clenched between his teeth, and I had to give him snaps for being such a fan of tobacco that he hadn't tossed the thing away during the melee.

And then my foot caught against a bit of the sidewalk that was cracked and had shifted so that it was about an inch higher than the rest of the walkway. I sprawled forward, catching myself so my nose didn't splat against the pavement but scraping my hands and knees pretty badly. I scrambled to my feet quickly, but I could hear that my delay had worked in Stumpenhorst's favor. His clomping footsteps were dangerously close. My car—or rather, my stepfather's Merc—was in sight, though, and I darted toward it. I threw open the door and got in, sensing Stumpenhorst was almost within grabbing distance.

I was right. Just as I was swinging the door shut, he threw something at me. I didn't see what it was, but as it went past me and into the backseat, I didn't worry about it. I was more concerned with fishing out the keys and getting the hell out of there.

Stumpenhorst pounded his fists against the window. "Come on out of there, you coward!" His face was twisted in anger, and I realized I'd seen that angry face recently. It had been Stumpenhorst I'd seen out the window when Tony and I had been about to make a bed go squeaky squeaky squeaky. The same evil glare. The same rage. The same look in the eyes that said "There's rage inside here. Anger, rage, and not much else. Thought process minimal."

I smiled as the engine purred into life. I gave Stumpenhorst a little wave as I pulled away from the curb, and I saw, as the car put more and more of a distance between us, him running after me until the futility of his chase sank into his brain and he gave up, standing in the street. He looked like a little boy who had been cheated out of pulling the wings off a fly when the fly, deciding that this wasn't an activity that was conducive to his health, buzzed off.

My heart took several blocks to resume normal functions, and it wasn't until I was nearly back at the Weasley homestead that I realized I was sitting forward and so tense that my knuckles were doing the white thing against the steering wheel. Taking a deep breath, I told myself to calm down. My head was doing some Sherlock Holmes deductions as I navigated Rockford's streets.

I deduced Stumpenhorst had followed Tony to the Phantom Lady Inn, and it had been he who had climbed the tree outside my window in order to spy on us. But the text from Tony, begging me to meet him in the park? Ah, Watson, that text had *not* come from Tony but this same Stumpenhorst. When Tony and I had been out searching the grounds, he had thought he'd dropped something. That something must have been his cell phone. And Stumpenhorst had confiscated it. Tony had told me he couldn't find his phone, and I had just assumed he'd located it when I received the text. The child's play of logical deduction.

Rat Bastard

I was pretty pleased with figuring this out, but then as I approached my mom's house, my heart gave another lurch and my muscles clenched all over again. It was likely that, by now, the stepmonster would be home from his office, and that meant I would shortly be bearding the dreaded Dollings in his den.

I pulled into the drive. There were several lights on in the house, but no klaxons blazing and no stepfather standing on the front porch armed with a shotgun. I pulled past the dead Corvette and activated the automatic garage door opener. As it rose, I said a little prayer.

And Lady Luck was smiling on me. Or at least she wasn't, at present, kicking me in the nads. The stepmonster hadn't come home yet! There were the same number of automobiles present as when I'd left!

My eyes watered with thankful tears as I parked the Mercedes. My hand shook as I took the key out of the ignition, and I realized as I got out that I was famished. I hadn't eaten for hours, and suddenly I had a hankering for Burger King. I could almost smell the flame-broiled burgers. I sniffed. Weirdly, I really *could* smell something akin to burgers cooking. Rita must have scorched the evening meal. She'd be in big trouble, and I felt a pang for her. Not everyone could have the Weasel luck.

I had barely stepped away from the Merc when a car pulled into the driveway, blinding me with its headlights. Okay, I was caught in the garage with the door still open, but Dollings wouldn't know I had been driving his car. I had a story ready, so with a confident swagger I stepped out of the garage.

Dollings had parked next to my Corvette, and he slammed his door shut as he glared at me. Because the light from the garage was behind me, I couldn't see his face properly, but in his case that's a plus. "What," he demanded, "are you doing here?"

"My car has something wrong with it," I said, oozing nonchalance. I put my hands in my pockets and strode toward him, not because I liked being in his proximity, but because I didn't want him getting closer to the garage where he could hear the ticking of the Merc's engine as it cooled.

"What do you mean? Won't it start?"

There was something odd about his attitude. When I'd last been in the stepmonster's presence, it had been an even-money bet he was going to leap on me and tear me limb from limb. Now he seemed almost… well, not kind, because that would have been impossible for him, but there was there was almost sympathy in his tone. This made me wary.

Wary and hungry. The hunger pangs were hitting the high notes, going for the crescendo. The Burger-King smell intensified. I could almost taste the yummy burgers and crispy fries. My stomach gurgled, partly from hunger and partly as a warning not to get too close to Dollings. He might just be lulling me into a false sense of security so I'd get within throttling distance.

"Makes an odd groaning sound when you turn the key," I told him.

He nodded sagely, patting my car's hood. "I'll take a look at it. It might just be the battery. We can hook it up to the charger." Here he paused, and even in the light available I could see he was uncomfortable and struggling to find words. "Look here, Weasel, I need to apologize to you."

My eyes popped, and alarms went off in my head. He'd never, that I could recall, called me Weasel before, and he certainly had never apologized for anything ever in his life. This included his birth, which he really needed to apologize to the world at large for.

He went on. "Yesterday I may have come across a little strong. I said things in the heat of the moment that I didn't mean."

A little strong? That was like saying Hurricane Katrina was a tad breezy. I would have said something, but his words had robbed me of speech.

"I think," the stepmonster said, "that we both got a little carried away. I've talked this over with your mother, and she agrees that, while we both deplore… dislike, I should say… your lifestyle, that you are who you are and that there is nothing we can do about that."

I was waiting for him to whip out an AK-47 and start spraying bullets, screaming "So take this, you little bastard! Bwah ha ha!" He didn't. "Okay," I said, drawing out both syllables.

"So, you can keep your car. We'll get it working again."

I had a sudden, horrible vision of him coming up and putting his arm around me in a fatherly manner. Instinctively, I took a half step back. "Okay," I repeated, wondering just when I'd stepped into the Twilight Zone.

"And about your allowance, I... do you smell something burning?"

I sniffed. "I do. Smells like Burger King."

The stepmonster shook his head, dismissing the digression. "Anyway, I hope we can find some common ground. We'll never be friends, I'm sure you'll agree, but perhaps we can find a way to exist together."

"Um... okay." Okay. Good word. Nice, safe, and noncommittal.

And then he did it. He walked up to me and, while he didn't fold me in an embrace, he placed a hand on my shoulder. It seemed to pain him as much as it confused me. He must have found it hard to look me in the eye, so he glanced down at our shoes. "You're a pain, Patrick," he said. "A thorn in my side, but some people seem to like you."

"Okay," I said. So far the word had done right by me, and I wasn't ready to expand the vocabulary as yet, not until I knew what Dollings was doing. Something was up his sleeve; that much was sure.

Dollings tried to smile. The creep factor went up several notches. "I was talking with Cicely Talbot earlier today."

Ah. So that's what had caused his sudden change of... well, not heart, as he didn't have one, so we'll go with mind. "Oh?" I asked. Oh. The offshoot of the conversational okay. Still noncommittal and safe.

"As you know, she's just finished her biography of Charlotte Winston and is looking for a publisher. She was going to go with—I really do smell something burning, don't you?—Parsons Press, but they're being difficult over royalties."

Charlotte Winston, you'll remember, was my friend Jake's great aunt. She was quite a force in Illinois politics at one time, rubbing elbows with presidents and congressmen and foreign potentates and the like. She was always running to and fro, jabbering with the Powers That Be in northern Illinois. Not so long ago she died, which greatly slowed down the to-ing and fro-ing. Her death would, however, deliver a sock-o finish to Cicely's biography, which no doubt needed a good moment or two to relieve the doldrums.

"Oh?" I said.

"Yes," the stepmonster replied. He seemed to be a little annoyed with my one-syllable answers, but he was leading up to something, and he was trying not to let his irritation show. "She now thinks that, quite rightly of course, Dollings Press is the best home for her book." The stepmonster scratched at his ear. "She asked about you."

"I bet she did," I muttered. In the past, she'd camped outside my doorstep, tried to convince me I was engaged to her, and even had flowers delivered to me during one of my classes. Why not ask about me? She probably stopped strangers on the street, asking them their views on one Patrick Carrington Weasley.

He ignored my interjection. "She's quite fond of you," he said. I had the feeling that mentally he added, "Lord knows why." His throat made a weird sort of barking sound, and I realized he was trying to chuckle. "Now, I know you aren't her biggest fan—"

"There are psychiatric wards that have her picture on the wall. 'Have you seen this woman?'"

Dollings cleared his throat, probably to erase the memory of that aborted chuckle. "Be that as it may, it would mean a great deal to me if you would help me clinch the deal. You know, take her out for a night on the town. Wine and dine her."

Rat Bastard

I shook my head. "At present, I could barely afford to take her to Burger King." I really had flame-broiled burgers on the brain. "And, last I checked, the wine list at Burger King was sparse in the extreme."

The stepmonster tried on his apologetic face. It wasn't much better than his normal mug. "Yes, about that. Perhaps I was a bit hasty in taking away your allowance. Maybe we could reach a compromise?"

With Tony's Christmas present firmly in mind, I asked, "What did you have in mind?"

"A reinstatement of your allowance, of course. I never will like your lifestyle, and I wish you'd consider going to one of our church's Enlightenment Camps, where they bring you back to the straight and narrow, so to—"

I laughed, loudly and giving it the hollow treatment. "One of those ex-gay thingies? That's all hogwash, I hope you know. It's been shown that—"

He could see his words had caused me to get a little heated, so he raised his hands in a calming gesture. "It was just a suggestion. But if you could see your way to take Cicely out—"

"In writing."

"Pardon?"

"My allowance. I want it in writing, nice and legal, that you won't be able to rescind it at your whim."

His lip twitched, but he nodded and stuck out his hand for me to shake. "Done."

I was wondering if I had enough leverage to ask for an increase in the allowance department and was just about to open my mouth when I saw he was glancing behind me.

"You're," he said, pausing as something caught his eye, "… on fire."

I've had a lot of guys give me compliments over the years (if you like them tall, pale, and willowy, I'm your guy!), and a lot of them have even told me, usually when seeing me on the dance floor at the Twenty-One Club, that I was "on fire," but it wasn't something I was expecting to come out of the stepmonster's mouth. "Pardon?"

"My car," he said, his voice tiny with disbelief. "My Mercedes. It's on fire."

I turned and looked into the garage. What he said was true. Flames were dancing about in the backseat, getting quite jiggy, as flames are wont to do. Even as I looked, the fire began to spread to the front seat, there not being enough elbow room in the back.

My mind boggled. How the heck…. And then it occurred to me. Reading all those Sherlock Holmes stories makes one figure things out from the clues presented, and it occurred to me what must have happened.

Gates Stumpenhorst (still can't get over that name. I mean, the Stumpenhorst you're born with, can't work around that, but Gates? What the hell!) had thrown something at me as I'd gotten into the car. It had gone into the backseat. He'd been smoking a cigarette. Cigarette wasn't in his mouth when he'd been pounding on the window in futile fury. Therefore what he'd thrown had been the cigarette. Said cigarette had nestled against Mom's rags she'd used to clean her painting supplies. Oily rags had slowly smoldered until they had eventually erupted into flames. QED.

This was an oops moment if there ever was one. Although, really, not entirely my fault. I mean, who sticks paint rags in the back of a nearly new, very expensive Mercedes-Benz? Just asking for people to toss lit cigarettes back there, if you ask me.

"Got a fire extinguisher?" I asked, wanting to be helpful.

"My Mercedes," Dollings muttered. "My beautiful Mercedes."

Not helpful at all. I was just about to hop inside the house and get an extinguisher when I heard a distant siren. Some neighbor had, it seemed, looked out their window and noticed the car was going up in flames. Nice of them, of course, but it was going to be really hard to convince old Deputy Sheriff Bradley I wasn't an arsonist if he ever heard about this little incident.

Rat Bastard

I should have, in retrospect, taken the keys to my mother's Kia Rio. Had that gone up in flames, I would have been doing the motoring world a favor.

Chapter Eight

IT WAS December eighteenth, and I was at my post, the desk of the Phantom Lady Inn, and was quickly running out of things to do. I had long since finished *The Hound of the Baskervilles* and had, in fact, engulfed *The Murder of Roger Ackroyd* by A. Christie (didn't see that ending coming!) and had polished off *Clouds of Witness* by Dorothy Sayers. I hadn't delved into the Sayers oeuvre before and was fascinated by her detective, Lord Peter Wimsey, so much so that I tried modeling a monocle in the mirror to see if I could carry one off. Not having a monocle handy, I had to use the cap off a milk jug, but it was enough to let me know it was a daft idea. I flipped a coin to see if my next book would be another Lord Peter or if I should gobble up *The Return of Sherlock Holmes.* Holmes won, so Lord Peter's next adventure would have to wait.

Taking a break from reading, and as we'd had one customer check in that morning and, if the past was anything to go by, that was going to be it for the day as far as work went, I played some Angry Birds and then went on to solitaire.

"Wait a minute!" some of you may be saying. "You left us with you standing in the drive with your stepfather's car burning away! Did you wiggle your way out of getting blamed for that?"

Let me take you back. The dramatis personae were, you will recall, the stepmonster and me. Well, us and assorted firemen. The fire department was pretty quick at putting out the blaze, leaving behind the scent of charred car. During their visit, the stepfather held up fairly well, although he was prone to muttering curses to the gods who are supposed to watch over defenseless Mercedes-Benzes. When a nice fireman, who seemed to be in charge of the Merc-dousing operation and, it must be said, was nowhere near as hunky as firemen are generally depicted to be, questioned the stepmonster as to the cause of the blaze, all Dollings could do was whimper a bit and say he had no idea. Naturally, I kept my big trap shut during these proceedings.

Another fireman—this one, while not in the hunky category, was at least doable in a pinch if you could overlook his potbelly and his frankly horrendous mustache—reported it had been soiled rags in the backseat which had ignited. On hearing this, the first fireman gave my stepfather a look that pretty much said "Well, there you go." If you're going to leave rags in the back of your car, you deserve an inferno or two.

After they'd gone, the stepmonster and I stood in the middle of the driveway for a few minutes, he because his legs didn't want to move and me because I wanted to make sure I wasn't going to get the blame.

"I don't understand," he muttered, "how this could have happened."

"You heard the man," I said. "Mom's rags went whoosh."

"But something must have ignited them."

Well, yes. A cigarette butt, thrown at me by G. Stumpenhorst, ex-boyfriend of Tony and a loony of the first degree, but I wasn't going to offer that explanation. "Spontaneous combustion," I suggested.

"I beg your pardon?"

"You hear about it all the time. Usually it's some guy sitting in a mobile home, dressed in dirty jeans and a dingy wifebeater, drinking a beer and watching NASCAR. Then all of a sudden he's a Roman candle. When the smoke clears, you have a charred hunk of redneck, but the chair and even the beer can are hardly singed. One of Mother Nature's great mysteries. Or maybe she just doesn't like NASCAR."

I could tell by his dubious expression he wasn't swallowing the spontaneous combustion theory. In fact, I thought I detected a temporary gleam in his eye as he wondered if I could have in some way been responsible. But no. His face fell as he couldn't come up with a likely scenario. "When you went in, did you use the automatic garage door opener?"

"Why, yes."

"Perhaps," he said with a frown, "the mechanism sparked and that spark got into the car and started the fire."

And he thought spontaneous combustion was unlikely? Oh, yeah, a spark went *through* the roof of the Merc and set the rags aflame. "That's probably what happened," I said. "I'd write the manufacturer a strongly worded letter if I were you."

For now, at least, my hide was saved.

WHILE WE'RE doing the catch-up game, I had finished my finals— did rather well, in my opinion—and was now working full time at the inn. I was pretty much living there too, having gathered some of my junk from my apartment in Rockford and made the small room upstairs in the inn rather cozy. Plus, it was a boon to just be able to get up, shower, dress, go downstairs, and be at work.

And, while we currently only had two guests (count 'em, two!), we had several bookings coming up (things were looking up for Mr. Rivers!), and I had suggested to the stepmonster, who was having a big Christmas bash for his authors and staff, to schedule his party at the Phantom Lady. While I disliked having the stepmonster in close proximity, I wanted to do right by Mr. Rivers and drum up some business. Seconds after making the suggestion, regret sank in, but by then it was too late.

Rat Bastard

A new employee was added to the fold, a rather nice-looking youngster named Austin. Kind of hunky, with dark hair and sparkling eyes and a good, solid build. If I had been on the market, I'd have made a play for him. Just as well I wasn't, as he turned out to be straight and had a weird, high-pitched laugh that set my teeth on edge. But still, it was nice to have some eye candy around.

We'd decorated the hell out of the place, putting wreaths up, hanging the obligatory mistletoe, and dotting the front lawn with animated, lighted reindeer and a blow-up Santa. A big old tree dominated the lobby, festooned with garlands, lights, and baubles. Bing Crosby's "White Christmas" was playing, and even Mother Nature had done her bit and snowed overnight, giving us a few inches of fluffy white.

With all the yuletide cheer surrounding me, you'd think it would be hard to be glum. But glum was what I was. For one, what with finals and work, I'd hardly been able to see Tony at all. Sure, we'd texted and spoke on the phone together like there was no tomorrow, but the soul was yearning to actually *see* him. Kiss him. And, to be blunt, pump him and see if I could make him squeak like a balloon.

In addition to the lack of Tony in my life, I had also (insert groan here) called the dreaded Talbot and set up a date. The conversation had gone something like this:

Me: (disappointed that she'd answered the phone) "Oh. Hello."

Cicely: "Weasel!"

Me: "Um. Yes."

Cicely: "It's so nice to hear from you!"

Me: "I can imagine. Anyway, do you want to go out Saturday night? Dinner and a movie. Something action-filled and bloody. The movie, I mean."

Cicely: "Sounds fantastic!"

Me: "I thought we'd go to that new Chinese place downtown."

Cicely: "Great!"

Her enthusiasm was annoying me. Me: "It hasn't gotten very good reviews. One critic's entire review was just the word 'no.' And I hear several people have gotten food poisoning from eating there."

Cicely: "Well, we can always go somewhere else."

Me: "But I've booked."

Cicely: "I'm sure it will be fine."

Me: "Cicely, I'm still gay."

Cicely: (laughing) "No, you're not!"

Me: "Pretty sure I am. Definition of gay—sleeping with the same sex. I pretty much fit that bill."

Cicely: "It's just a phase."

Me: A very long phase. With no end in sight. "Really, I'm gay."

Cicely: "Well, you won't be after Saturday night!"

After a phone call like that, can you blame me for being glum?

I was just settling into the Holmes story "The Adventure of the Empty House" when the cook, Sammy, ambled by. He eyed me critically. "You look down," he said.

"I was going with glum, but down will do."

"Why so?"

"Got a date Saturday night."

"With Tony? I thought you and he were still hot for each other."

"We are. This date is with a girl named Cicely Talbot."

He stared at me. "You're a very confusing young man."

"It's been said."

Rat Bastard

Sammy leaned against the counter, oozing boredom. Breakfast was over, and I don't suppose he had a lot of cleaning up after serving a whole two people. "So," he asked, "have you got that ring for Tony yet?"

With a small staff, everyone knew everyone's business. "Getting it Monday, I think." I was waiting for Dollings to dish out the allowance before making my purchase, and I think he was waiting out doling out the good stuff until he was sure I'd honor my end of the bargain and go out with the loony. The money I was making at the inn wasn't bad but hardly in the ring-buying range. As it was, I still wasn't going to be able to put down as much of a down payment as I'd hoped. The ring I'd selected was a beaut, though, and I knew Tony would go ape over it.

Sammy was about to reply when we both heard the front door begin to open. There's a little bell over the door that jangles, and I think the bell was as surprised as we were that it was getting a workout. The guy who entered was buried under a heavy coat, and his face was nearly covered by the long scarf wrapped around it. Sammy and I both snapped to attention as the newcomer stamped snow off his shoes and unwrapped his face.

"Goodness, it's getting cold out there!" said a muffled yet strangely familiar voice. Then he unwrapped enough of the visage to reveal it was just my friend Jake. Seeing who it was, Sammy relaxed and went back to slouching against the front desk.

I was pleased to see my buddy, as the last few days at the inn had been frankly dull, and it would be good to have a friendly face on the premises. The best conversations I'd had lately had been, frankly, with Rodney the dog. Mrs. Kendall was still in residence, although why she was staying on none of us could figure out. She rarely left her room, save for going out to walk Rodney. And even then, once the snow had started to fall, she'd left that chore to me, as she didn't like going out in the cold. Rodney wasn't fond of it either, and when he trotted out in it, he'd glance back at me with that sort of "Can you get rid of this shit?" look on his face.

"What are you doing here?" I asked Jake as he deposited coat, scarf, and one of those weird caps with the long tassels that hang down nearly to the shoulders onto the coat rack.

"I thought I'd come by, see how you were doing, chat with the uncle… that sort of thing. Partially because I haven't seen you in ages, but mostly because the boyfriend is off seeing his folks for an early Christmas and I didn't have anything else to do. Didn't Uncle Eric tell you I was coming?"

"He hadn't mentioned it."

"Probably forgot."

"He's good at that."

Actually, Mr. Rivers was a master at forgetting. Just the previous day I'd had to remind him twice that it was payday, and, while it seemed like robbery to expect money for doing so little, the agreement was that he'd actually give me money for standing around. Hovering over the checkbook with pen in hand, he had hesitated. "How much am I paying you?"

I told him, adding in a small raise for myself. After all, we had two guests now.

He frowned. "Are you sure that's enough? That's what we'd agreed on? It doesn't seem very much. As you've been doing so well, let me give your salary a bit of a bump." And he'd added another fifty cents an hour onto the quarter raise I'd given myself. Just goes to show you.

Jake nodded at the cook as he ambled up to the desk. "Sammy, right?"

"Yep." The two of them shook hands. Being sans friends for several days, not to mention sans Tony, I wasn't having any of that mere handshake stuff as a greeting, so I went around the desk and engulfed Jake in a bear hug. When I'd released him, he laughed as he blew on his hands.

Rat Bastard

"That's one way to warm up," he said as he did a little shivery jig. "It really is cold out there! And the snow is starting to really fall!"

"You call this cold?" Sammy asked disdainfully. The cook, I'd learned, was from Minnesota originally, and if there was something Minnesotans liked to talk about it was snow. If you're ever at a party and you're stuck in a corner with a Minnesotan who won't converse, just mention the word snow to him. Warning: he won't shut up after that. He'll regale you with tales of the blizzard of '03 and then go on to try to convince you his grandfather actually became a snowman going out to get the mail one day but hadn't moved fast enough. Snow and weather in general were topics dear to the heart of Sammy the cook. He went on. "Why, it's still in the upper twenties out there! That's not cold. Almost a Minnesota summer. You Illinois boys just can't handle a proper winter."

Jake stopped blowing on his hands and put them in his pockets instead. "Well, I guess it's not really that bad out there. Just not used to it yet. The cold, I mean. We get some pretty big snows here in northern Illinois too, you know."

Sammy uttered a pshaw and waved dismissively at Jake. "Up in Minnesota, boys your age are still wearing shorts in weather like this. They'd laugh at seeing you coming in all trussed up like that."

Jake sputtered a little, his ego bruised. "Well… I just… well… it was the only coat I had to wear."

It was a nice try, but the fact that he'd had to wrap his face like Claude Rains removing bandages in *The Invisible Man* detracted from his excuse. Sammy didn't buy it either, and he laughed hollowly. "You boys just can't take the cold here. Why, even the gal this place is named after had more chutzpah than you guys. She ran around in the snow in her undies!"

"Of course," I noted, "she was supposedly a ghost and therefore wouldn't feel the cold."

My point seemed to irk the cook. "Still," he said simply.

Jake nodded toward me. "I bet Weasel here can take the cold better than anyone up in your precious Minnesota. Did you know he once swam in the fountain at Purdue University when it was nearly iced up?"

"True," I said. "Of course, that was back in the days when I was minoring in drinking. I believe I was enacting a scene from *Titanic* for some friends of mine. I was playing both the Leonardo DiCaprio and Kate Winslet parts. Some said I was a better Rose than Winslet, although they may have been drunk at the time and their judgment slightly impaired."

Sammy seemed unimpressed. "You couldn't do what the Phantom Lady did. You boys are too soft."

"What, you mean streak around in my underwear in the snow? I wouldn't have a problem with that, if the incentive was right."

"A hundred bucks says you can't do it," Sammy said, slapping the counter for emphasis.

"You're on," I said immediately.

"Dressed," he added, "as the Phantom Lady."

In my mind, I had pictured a little jaunt in my boxers and tennis shoes, so I adjusted the picture and added a bra. Warmer. Not by much, but warmer. "It may surprise you to know," I had to say, dashing the cook's dreams, "that just because I'm gay doesn't mean I keep a supply of women's wigs and underwear handy."

"He does make a good-looking woman, though," Jake said.

It was true. I made a handsome female. The frame, though thoroughly masculine, transforms when you stick a dress and a wig on me and has even made the straightest construction-worker type drool a little. When I was fourteen, I'd chosen to be Britney Spears for Halloween. Pre-crazy Britney, of course, before the shaved head and Kevin Federline. I'd even made the captain of the football team look twice. And more recently, I'd masqueraded as my cousin, "Kitty," causing at least one burly straight man to fall in love with a woman who didn't exist. Still, I was hesitant to don yet another wig.

The world can have too much of a good thing. "I don't know," I said.

"Two hundred," Sammy replied.

"Done."

Well, for one, I could put down even more on the ring down payment. And I figured no one would see me anyway, being out in the middle of nowhere during a snowstorm.

Shows you what I know.

IT WAS still early evening, but, as we were close to the solstice, the sun had long since retired for the day. The snow had stopped, and the clouds had moved on, letting the moon shine down on the surroundings. We had gone to Mandy, the housekeeper, to borrow one of her bras, and on hearing what we were up to, she decided she had to join us. The wig, a mass of blonde tresses, was supplied by Sammy himself. When we'd questioned him, he shrugged.

"I used to do drag. What, did you think your generation invented it?"

So there I was, dressed in wig, a bra too big for me, panties (also from Sammy's old days), and my Nikes. Why Sammy had a wig and panties but no bras no one thought to ask. Truth be told, I was already a little chilled in the getup, and I hadn't even stepped outside yet. By this time the new guy, Austin, had joined us—luckily no one else. It would have been embarrassing to have Mr. Rivers among the well-wishers. After all, one strives to keep an air of responsibility and decorum with one's employer, and having them see you in women's underwear doesn't really fit the bill.

Mandy pulled out her smartphone as I was about to head out, but I shook my head. "No pictures," I said. "And no video. I don't want to end up all over the Internet. That wasn't part of the deal."

She put her phone away reluctantly. "Okay," she muttered.

Jake patted me on the back. "Good luck, Weasel."

"Thank you."

"You have to jog down to the river and back," Sammy said, reiterating the agreement we'd already gone over several times. "And you have to stick to the side of the road. No hiding behind trees or something if a car comes by."

"Yes, I know." Suddenly I just wanted to get the thing over with and pocket the money. Taking a deep breath, I opened the door and bolted out onto the porch. Jake, Sammy, Austin, and Mandy followed me, but they stayed on the porch and watched as I darted out onto the front lawn. I could hear Mandy giggling and Austin laughing his bizarre laugh behind me. Jake shouted encouragement. Encouragement was nice, as the snow, while not deep, was already making my feet chilled, and there was a slight night breeze that wanted to seep its way into my bones.

I don't know if you've ever run down a road at night wearing only a bra, panties, and basketball shoes, not to mention a fluffy blonde wig. Probably you haven't. From experience I can tell you it leaves you feeling a little… exposed. I made quick work of the lawn and made it to the road. Sucking in cold air was making my lungs complain a bit, but I found if I kept up a good pace, I didn't feel the chill too badly. I ran by the side of the road. No traffic. I was getting into the zone, and even the cold and the fact that snow had somehow found its way into my shoes couldn't slow me down. I was on fire! One with nature! One with the night! I felt like I was in the limelight, on a stage, mesmerizing an audience.

And then I realized that I *was* in lights. Headlights, to be precise. A car had come up behind me.

I flashed a quick backward glance. The inn was just a black shape in the distance, and I was pleased I'd gone farther than I'd thought. I wasn't so pleased that the car had spotted me and was slowing down. I was even less pleased when I heard the whoop of a siren and saw red-and-blue lights begin to flash. I continued my jog at a slower pace and put a smile on my face. Surely the cop would see this as the harmless prank that it was, and we'd have a good laugh before he sent me on my way.

Rat Bastard

A bright light hit me as the driver of the squad car turned his side lamp my way. I blinked and shielded my eyes as I slowed to a halt.

"Excuse me, miss. Is there a problem?"

I knew the voice. The driver of the squad car was none other than Deputy Bradley.

Chapter Nine

I ONCE had an argument, one of many, with Mrs. Climthorpe. I had written an essay which she taken offense to. My subject was King Solomon, which you'd have thought would have been right up old Climthorpe's alley, as the only book she thought worth reading was the Bible. My essay took a whimsical turn, though, when I went into discussing Solomon's wives. I don't know if you know this, but according to the Bible, the good king had 700 wives and 300 concubines, which you have to admit is overdoing things a bit. I mean, even if he used a rotation system, wife number 700 must have almost forgotten about the dude by the time it came for her to visit the royal bedchamber. I believe I may have, in my essay, suggested she may have even complained a bit. "What, is it 967 BC already? I thought I was safe until 966!"

Climthorpe took a dim view of my project and graded it accordingly. When I complained, she told me in no uncertain terms that one shouldn't inject a little fun into the Bible. Serious stuff, she said. My position was that God had a pretty good sense of humor. You can't tell me that creating the duckbilled platypus didn't give him a giggle. And then there was my Uncle Frank, whose face looked like it had been constructed from leftover parts, sort of like a Mr. Potato Head.

I bring up Mrs. Climthorpe and Solomon and even Uncle Frank to illustrate a point. God enjoys a good chuckle. Otherwise he wouldn't have stuck me out on a road in the middle of the night wearing women's underwear and arranging for the one person to spot me being Officer Bradley. I mean, what are the odds? I guess a sheriff's deputy has to be *somewhere* on a chilly December evening, but did it have to be around Kennedy Hill Road while I was jogging in drag?

I acted quickly. I bolted.

"Wait! Miss! Wait!" I heard him calling.

Like that was going to happen. I don't believe I've ever run faster, in fact. Fear gave me that extra oomph in my step, so I made good time. I didn't want to find out what the man's reaction would be once he'd gotten a better look at the jogger he'd found, but I assumed he'd find some reason to throw me in a jail cell for the night because of some obscure Byron ordinance that says you can't run nearly naked along Kennedy Hill Road because it might disturb the local wildlife, or some such nonsense. To be truthful, I didn't give it much thought. I just ran.

"Miss!" The voice sounded closer. I chanced a glance backward. Bradley had parked his car and was chasing after me. I could see the light from his flashlight bobbing up and down as his beefy body tried to keep up with my gazelle-like strides.

"Shit!" I cursed aloud. You don't want to use up energy by uttering things when you're in these situations, but I felt the word needed to be expressed.

And to make matters worse, Mandy's bra was *really* pinching my upper ribs. The thing seemed to have grown smaller in the cold, shrinking to uncomfortable levels.

My lungs were beginning to ache. I knew I was running out of steam, and that before long, the long arm of the law would catch up with me. I couldn't let that happen.

I reached the end of the road, where Kennedy Hill meets up with the scenic Illinois Highway Two. I ran across the highway. There were at least two cars, one coming each way, but I easily got across the road without either of them having to slam on the brakes. Then I was down the embankment and at the edge of the Rock River. I looked back, feeling like a rabbit a pack of dogs have got their eyes on. The beam from Bradley's flashlight was off in the distance but too close for comfort. I braced myself and almost dove into the water. Then I had a vision of a doctor saying the word hypothermia several times while shaking his head and saying bits of me had frozen off and were presumably now fish food and he was so sorry. So I scrambled up a tree. I made quick work of it and made a lot of noise doing so, but it was nothing compared to the noise coming from the road. There were horns honking, doors slamming, and people shouting. Apparently one or two of the drivers had spotted the pale but strangely sexy woman with the long blonde hair darting across the road and had stopped to investigate.

"Did you see what I saw? A naked woman!"

"She disappeared into thin air!"

Well, that person was wrong on two counts. She was a he, and he was freezing his tokus off in a tree along the banks of the Rock River.

Then I heard Bradley's voice. He was more than a little winded. "Did you guys see that woman?"

"See her? She ran right in front of our car!"

"She vanished right before us! I'd always heard this road was haunted."

"I've never heard that."

"It was even in the newspapers, years back. Some female ghost. Think that's what we saw?"

Bradley was still breathing heavily. "She has to be around here somewhere."

I saw the flashlight beam search the bank before the light began to stray over the water. I held my breath, praying he wouldn't think of looking up. I could see that a small crowd had gathered below me, with Bradley and a couple of guys being much too close to my tree for comfort.

The branch I was on was nice and sturdy but much too low for my liking. I was only about two feet above the head of Bradley, and if he looked up he'd hardly fail to notice that nestled among the branches was a lanky stud dressed in women's undergarments, shivering his ass off. It was too much to hope he'd mistake me for an owl, because I've seen owls, and none of them resemble a six-foot-tall blond guy in a bra and panties. Even if I hooted.

"There's no sign of anyone," one of the motorists said. "She vanished!"

The deputy's flashlight played across the surface of the water and then onto the bank. He swept the area with the beam, finding nothing of note. "She must be here somewhere. I was right behind her!"

A new person joined the throng, this one a female. "What's going on? Has there been an accident?"

"A ghost! The Phantom Lady of Kennedy Hill Road has made a reappearance!"

"I'd always heard this road was haunted." This was a new voice, who obviously didn't know this same phrase had already been used before his arrival. "Did you actually see her?"

Another voice joined in. "She ran right in front of my car! Well, when I say ran, I should say floated. I swear she wasn't actually touching the pavement! And you could see right through her! It was like she was mist or something!"

"I saw the same thing! There was like a mist around her!"

"I must say, she had big knockers for a ghost." This statement was met with a short, uncomfortable silence. "Just saying," the speaker added.

My leg was cramping up, and my teeth wanted to do their impression of castanets clicking together, but I forced myself to stay still.

Eventually it became apparent that the ghost was indeed gone and the thrill seekers weren't going to catch another glimpse of that frankly fabulous body, and the small crowd began to disperse. I heard muffled talking and the sounds of people getting back into their vehicles. Bradley, refusing to believe a scantily clad woman could elude him, stayed behind, playing his flashlight beam over the same territory again and again. Eventually even he gave up and returned to the road.

I waited, making sure I gave him and everyone else ample chance to go on their way. Finally I lowered my aching body out of the tree and dropped to the ground. It wasn't the best dropping out of a tree I've ever done, and I sprawled forward on my hands and knees, allowing some skin to get up close and personal with snow and, in the case of my right knee, a rock. I stood, cursing, and brushed myself off.

I don't know if you're familiar with Richard III. He was one of Shakespeare's dudes. Anyway, during a battle, his horse was killed, and there he was, in the midst of a skirmish, on foot when everyone else was on a steed. Famously, he yelled out, "A horse! A horse! My kingdom for a horse!" which, you have to admit, was a pretty good rate for a horse, especially in those days. I mean, back then you could probably buy a horse for a bundle of carrots and a packet of mud. So a kingdom was a nice offer. I didn't have a kingdom, but I'd have given everything I owned—and I mean everything, even my signed photograph of John Barrowman as Captain Jack from *Torchwood*—if at that moment someone had wandered by with a nice, warm blanket.

I thought about jogging back to the inn, but after a couple of steps I realized my knee had been grazed and bruised by the rock and was in no mood for jogging, so I limped as quickly as I could in the direction of the inn.

All in all, I've had better nights.

Chapter Ten

I'VE ALSO had better mornings. I awoke around nine, groggy and confused. I sat up, trying to remember who I was and why my bones ached so. Then it all came flooding back. The jog in the snow. The near catch by Deputy Bradley. The lonely and cold trek back to the inn. The guffaws from my friend and coworkers when I returned, once they'd grabbed warm clothes for me and sat me down with some hot tea. I didn't join in on the laughter, as I was worried it would make my chest hurt even more. As it was, my lungs weren't speaking to me. Neither was my knee or most of the bones in my body. So I made an early night of it, snuggling under extra blankets until sleep overtook me. I think I dreamed of being dipped into a vat of ice cream.

I creaked out of bed and thought, for the briefest of moments, about taking some sort of pain reliever. Normally, I keep away from such medications. I'm one of those people who have an extreme reaction to pills. Take an Advil and I feel like jelly for hours. Those allergy capsules that promise they're nondrowsy? Snore city for me. I once took a Darvocet (prescribed by a doctor who didn't believe my protestations that I reacted badly to pain meds) and was convinced I was the reincarnation of Arthur Rimbaud and was running down the streets yelling for Paul Verlaine. My father was alive at the time, and he found me and carted me back to the doctor. Dad didn't think it was impossible that I really was the reincarnation of the poet Rimbaud, saying, "It's just the sort of silly ass thing my son would be." The doctor assured us I'd be fine, but I noticed he refused to be drawn into the debate as to whether or not I was Rimbaud's reincarnation. Considering how poorly I did in poetry in school, I'm thinking not.

So I groaned and decided against pain reliever. I dressed slowly and was just putting on my basketball shoes when there was a rapping at my chamber door.

"Come in," I said. It came out a hoarse, unintelligible croak, so I cleared my throat and tried again. The second attempt was a close approximation to human speech, enough to be understood by the person doing the rapping. It turned out to be Jake, who was grinning like a cat in a Lewis Carroll story.

"Uncle Eric wants to know if you can start your shift a little early today."

"It's my day off."

"And you expected my uncle to remember that?"

"You have a point there."

"And," Jake said, brandishing his cell phone, "you might get really busy this afternoon."

I rolled my eyes. "What, three guests at a time? Whatever will we do?"

"Already had two people call up to see if they could book rooms. I expect we'll have a full house by the end of the night."

That had me frowning. "Is a convention coming to town?"

Jake's grin reached epic proportions as he pointed his phone's screen at me. I got closer, and what I saw made me grab the phone out of his hands. He had been playing a video, and, while I only caught the tail end of it, what I saw made me blanch. And when you're as pale as I am, blanching isn't something that comes easily.

On the tiny screen was me, dressed in women's underwear, running alongside Kennedy Hill Road.

I gasped. Then I tried a whimper. Finally words came to me. "What is this?"

"The footage that Mandy took of you last night. Pretty good, isn't it? The moonlight really does make you look ghostly, plus she wasn't that close to you. She put it on YouTube last night. It's already had over seven hundred hits, and it's only been on a few hours. The Phantom Lady has returned!"

He took the phone out of my hands. I could only gape at him. "But I told her not to take any pictures or video!"

"Well, yeah. But you didn't think she'd pass up the opportunity, did you?" He punched the replay button, and the footage began again. "Honestly, I don't know why you're standing there looking like a fish, opening and closing your mouth like that. You can't tell it's you. It really does look like a ghostly figure, scampering alongside the road in the snow! This is just what the Inn needs. A reporter from *The Byron Chronicle* has already been by, so you'll be in tonight's paper, and Channel Thirteen News is sending out a crew to do a story."

"A reporter has been here already? That soon?"

"Not much happens in Byron. You can only write so many missing kitty stories before you start to want to stretch your writing muscles and sink your teeth into something a little more juicy."

I nodded. He had me there. "And you say people are starting to call and book rooms?"

"I expect we'll be full by this afternoon. And tonight they'll all be scanning the road for a sight of the Phantom Lady. The ghost already has her own Facebook page, by the way. I set that up myself, with a few grainy but spooky pictures of you doing your thing. I haven't checked yet to see how many likes the page has gotten so far."

I stared at him. "Facebook page?" Things clicked into place. "You set me up. You planned this whole thing."

At least Jake had the decency not to deny it. He gave me a semi-apologetic smile and said, "Well, Uncle Eric's place needed help, and I knew that way back when, when the Phantom Lady was being seen doing her nightly jogs, that people thronged to see her. I figured what the Phantom Lady Inn needed was a Phantom Lady, and as you will pop into women's clothes at the drop of a hat—"

"I've done it a few times!"

Jake raised an eyebrow. "I've known drag queens that don't don stuffed bras as often as you do. Regardless, the scheme has worked."

It had, indeed. I spent the next few hours checking people into the inn and fielding phone calls. Realizing that, with a full house, we might need a bigger staff than we currently had, Mr. Rivers made a few calls of his own and got extra housekeeping staff and a couple of people to wait tables. During a lull, he came down to the desk and checked to see how things were going.

"As of a half hour ago," I told him, "we're full for tonight. And tomorrow night."

He beamed. "I knew it was only a matter of time. Nothing like a ghost to keep your inn bustling!" A dreamy look crossed his face. "Maybe I'll call up one of the ghost-hunting television shows."

"I'd wait. After all, she's just made her first appearance in years. Maybe she was just flexing her muscles, making sure her running skills were still there, and won't be seen again for another thirty years or so."

Shaking his head, he said, "No, she's here in full force. She's been prowling around the house at night, although I haven't actually seen her. Probably uses this house as her HQ, a place where she rests up, and then when the urge hits her she darts down the road in her undies."

"Your trap hasn't caught anything yet?"

"Not yet, but I'm sure it will. She stole a pen of mine last night, you know. Nice silver pen. A Cross. Had my name inscribed on it."

"Maybe she had a note to write. She'll probably return it at her earliest convenience."

"I don't know. She hasn't returned anything else she's nicked. Bit of a kleptomaniac, our ghost. Still, if she keeps the guests coming like this, she deserves a pen or watch every now and then."

He pottered off after that, and I went back to answering phone calls. Mostly I had to break it to people that they couldn't get a room, although some just wanted information about the ghost sighting.

"No," I told more than one caller, "I didn't see the ghost myself. I hear, though, that she's got one fantastic bod."

Some callers, finding their hopes for a weekend room dashed, tried to book for the following week. I had to juggle a bit, as Daddy Dollings and several of his cronies had booked rooms for the middle of the week for the big Dollings Press Christmas bash, but that wasn't difficult. No mistakes were made, so the stepmonster wouldn't have to shack up with another guest, which would have been fairly nasty for said guest. I mean, would you?

After several hours of these calls, I was beginning to become bored with the whole thing and answered each ring with, "No, we don't have any rooms tonight, and no, I didn't see her. We still have some openings for next week. Can I put you down for Thursday?"

One caller answered with, "If you don't have any rooms for tonight, can I just sleep in your room with you?"

My heart did a jig. Tony! Immediately, my boredom fled. "God, it seems like years since I've heard your voice. You won't believe how nuts it is here, with all the ghost talk."

"I've seen the video on YouTube and I've liked the Facebook page. Apparently she hasn't set up a Twitter account yet."

"Give her time."

"It was hard to tell from the video, which could have been clearer, but I thought I recognized the figure."

"They could have used some camera tips from Zapruder," I said. When that remark was met with a confused silence, I added, "Zapruder was the guy that took the famous footage of the JFK assassination."

"You really do know the most arcane things, Weasel. You should go on *Jeopardy.* Anyway, I know we haven't had much luck getting together, what with one thing or another—"

"This is true."

"So I wiggled out of work tonight, since I knew you were free. So what do you say about a date?"

"I'd say, 'hello date'! What time, where, when, and should I do stretching exercises ahead of time?"

Tony laughed. "I get off at seven, so I should be able to get down there by around eight. You won't be busy running around nearly naked in the snow?"

"A one-off deal. It won't be repeated."

"Good. I'll see you tonight, then."

I was floating on air for quite a while after that. But for some reason the brain can't take too much happy, or at least mine can't, so I started to run the conversation with Tony over again in my head, analyzing it. Should I have apologized for not being more available? And then I started going further. Had I been wrong to take this job, robbing Tony and me of chances to get together? Was I flaunting the Boyfriend Zone? Luckily, the phone started ringing again, and I had to dash the hopes of even more ghost seekers and was kept busy enough checking people in and turning others away that I had to abandon my admittedly pointless worrying. What was done was done. I would prevail over the Boyfriend Zone, and Tony and I would be fine. The best way to smash the Boyfriend Zone is with a ring, and by Monday I'd have a doozy of one for Tony.

By five o'clock, I was putting the last key into the last guest's hand, and Jake sauntered up. "How are we doing?"

"We," I said, "are doing pretty good, both yours truly and the inn. Every guest has paid and been scooted into their room, and as soon as your uncle gets down here to relieve me, I'm off to have one heck of a night. All in all, a really good Friday."

"It's Saturday, you doofus."

"No, it isn't."

"It is."

There was a calendar on the desk, which I consulted. I didn't like what it told me. "It's Saturday."

"Kind of what I was trying to say."

The heart became leaden. "I'm supposed to go out with the dreaded Cicely tonight."

"Condolences."

"I don't want to go." Especially as I'd just made a date with Tony. Choice: go out with a semi-insane, clingy female who you don't even like and frankly terrifies you, or a gorgeous guy who you have high hopes for a meaningful relationship with. Not much of a choice.

"Don't go," Jake suggested.

Good advice. My hand started for the telephone. "I'll call and cancel."

"I would."

My hand hovered over the device. If I broke the date, it would get back to my stepfather. And he would go ballistic. And he'd withhold that moolah of mine. My fingers twitched, wondering what all the hovering was about. I still hesitated. Did I have any options?

Could I possibly do both?

"You're not phoning," Jake noted.

"I'm thinking."

"Don't strain yourself."

Was it possible to do a short date with Cicely and then have a long, enjoyable one with Tony? Maybe a short dinner with Cicely, and during said dinner come up with an excuse to cut the night short and then go see Tony. Oh, I'd make it possible. "I'd need a really good excuse," I said aloud.

"Dead grandmother? That's always a good one."

"She would tell Dollings, and he'd do a quick count of the grandparents and find that they're all alive and accounted for."

"Tell her you've fallen down the stairs. You do that a lot."

I shook my head. "She'd want to come and nurse me, kissing the bruises. No, what this excuse needs is a heavy dose of reality. The best excuses are rooted in the truth."

Just then Mr. Rivers arrived to relieve me, towing with him a young man he was going to train to help me run the front desk. Introductions were made, but I wasn't paying much attention. I needed to get to my room and change. I needed to look good, or at least presentable. Not for the Talbot wench, but for Tony. As soon as I was able, I darted for the stairs. Halfway up, Jake yelled after me.

"Hey, meet me at the bar before you head out. I want to introduce you to a new drink I've invented."

I paused at the landing. "I won't have time for drinks! I have a date!" Two, actually.

"Just a quick one. It'll buck you up. You'll need it, believe me."

I agreed, more to shut him up than anything else, and then sprinted to my room. I dressed quickly, and while donning my best duds I called Cicely, asking her to meet me at the restaurant. She agreed, sounding drippy and cheery. I tried to finish the call quickly, nearly hanging up on her, as she didn't seem to know the meaning of the words "gotta go, good-bye." It's not easy putting on fresh socks with a cell phone held to your ear by your shoulder, but I managed it. Finally our arrangements were made and I was dressed for a night out on the town. I don't own many button-down shirts, preferring T-shirts and jeans, but I did have a nice shiny blue thing that looked pretty good on me. I wore some black pants and black shoes to go with it. Simple but elegant.

I dashed back downstairs and headed for the bar, which was really just a lounge with a little wooden bar in the corner, although I must admit it was pretty well stocked. Standing behind the bar was someone I knew, Donald… or maybe it was Darren. They were twins, and although genetics claims they weren't identical, they were as near it as makes no difference. The last I had heard, they both were working at the same cafe, one the morning shift and the other worked the afternoon crowd, and they would wear the same name tag, so that if someone ate breakfast there and then later had lunch or dinner, they'd be amazed at the long hours the guy was putting in. Donald or Darren grinned when I approached.

"What," I asked, "are you doing here?"

"Working," the twin (we'll call him Donald because even if I asked which one it was I may not get the correct answer so it's best just to pick one and go with it) replied. "What with all the new arrivals, Jake's uncle panicked, thinking he didn't have enough employees, so Jake suggested me."

"And they put you at the bar? Isn't that a little like having a thief guard the vault?"

"Are you suggesting I can't dish out drinks without getting plastered myself?"

"I can smell the gin on your breath from here."

Donald shrugged. "Well, I had to sample the wares. Make sure none of it had spoiled or anything."

"Of course." I thought about letting him know that alcohol wasn't like milk, but I was in a hurry. I wanted to get my time with Cicely over with so I could, finally, spend some quality time with Tony. And this time there would be no spooky faces in windows or other calamities to interrupt us. "So," I said, turning to Jake, who had joined us, "what's this new drink you wanted me to try?"

"It's special," he said. Did I see him wink at Donald? Maybe I was just being paranoid. "I think you'll like it, though."

Donald must have had the concoction already prepared, for he simply reached under the bar and came up with a brandy snifter filled with a murky blue liquid decorated with a cocktail umbrella. I raised an eyebrow. "What is it, Romulan Ale? Why, Bones, I hope you know this stuff is illegal." My William Shatner impression isn't bad, but I could tell by Donald's reaction I could have been doing Bugs Bunny for all he knew.

"We can call it Romulan Ale if you like. It certainly has a kick to it."

I held up the snifter and peered at the contents. There were little bits of something floating within. "What's the white stuff?" I sat on one of the three bar stools available. Jake remained standing by my side.

"Try it! There's all kinds of stuff in there."

I took a sip. It had a sour taste and packed a bit of a jolt, but only because there were flavors fighting each other for supremacy. It was a colorful drink, but my taste buds were having a hard time figuring out what alcoholic beverages had been employed in the making of it. Gasoline, possibly, but no alcohol. Whatever else the drink did, it certainly cleared up the nasal passages. I coughed once or twice and then sneezed. I set the glass down and gave my eyes time to settle back into their sockets. "That's... interesting. What people don't drink, they can use to strip paint."

Jake frowned. "You've got to drink more of it than that! You just had a sip. Hardly enough to tell what it's like!"

"I can tell what it's like. It's like swallowing a shrew that's smoking a cigarette."

"That's just the first taste. After that, your taste buds get used to it."

"Get used to it? They're all waving the white flag as it is."

Jake pushed the vile drink closer to me. "Come on. Be a sport. At least you can tell me how I can fix it, make it better."

With a sigh, I took another drink. I sent a mental warning to my esophagus—brace yourself. Just to be fair, I made sure I swallowed a sizable amount of the potable. It probably would have been better just to have swallowed the cocktail umbrella. I gasped for air. "I think I know how you can fix this."

"How?"

"Add some vodka to it. Then forget everything else you've added and throw in some tonic water."

"That would just be a vodka and tonic."

"You catch on quick." I licked my lips, wincing. "There seems to be something grainy about it. What's in it, talcum powder?"

Jake grinned. "That's my secret ingredient."

"That's one secret you'll be allowed to take to your grave." I stood. "Well, I'd love to stay and die a slow, agonizing death by trying more of your experiments, but I've got a dinner date, and, much as I don't want to go, I have to. So have fun, boys!"

Donald—pretty sure it wasn't Darren—looked hurt. "That's all you're going to drink? I worked hard on that!"

"Much as I'd love to torture my tonsils," I said, letting the sarcasm drip, "I have to go or I'll be late."

Jake looked at the twin worriedly, and then at me. "You're not going on your date with Cicely, are you?"

"I have to."

I started to move away, but Jake stopped me by grabbing my elbow. "I really wouldn't."

Understanding dawned on me. "I get it. You guys thought if you got me drunk, I wouldn't go. Nice try."

"But you said you didn't want to go."

"I don't. But I have to, so I might as well get it over with."

A desperate gleam showed in Jake's eyes. "But should you drive after drinking? They're real strict around here, you know, about the legal limit."

"I had two sips, and I couldn't taste any alcohol. Sweat from a diseased warthog, yes, but no alcohol."

"You had two big sips. And that stuff's pretty potent. You just can't taste the alcohol."

I disengaged Jake's restraining hand. "Like I said, nice try, but I have to go."

Jake followed me as I made my way out of the lounge. "I may have done something really stupid."

"I'd say that was likely, knowing you."

"You see, I thought you wanted to get out of going out with Cicely."

"Well, yeah. You want to get out of having a root canal job done, but you have to endure it. Some things just have to be faced."

We'd gone out to the hall, and I got my hoodie off the coat rack, which, for the first time ever, was overflowing with garments. I guessed most of the coats and apparel belonged to new staff members such as Donald/Darren and Austin, as the guests surely would have taken their winter garments to their rooms with them. As I shuffled into my jacket, which was woefully too thin for the weather, Jake hovered.

"Maybe you shouldn't go. Maybe you should go lie down. Rest."

"Look, I appreciate your concern, but I want to get this over with. You see, after I spend a minimum time with Cicely, I'm going to spend maximum time with Tony. And hopefully some of that time we'll be naked and making squelchy noises."

Was it my imagination, or did Jake look sick? "I'd better tell you something."

"Tell me later. I have to head out."

"No, I really should tell you now."

Jake and I have been friends since we were toddlers, and I knew his delaying tactics when I saw them. "Later. Text me." And I was out the door before he could reply.

Chapter Eleven

IT WAS odd. As I drove the Corvette in the direction of State Street, where the restaurant, Beau Jardin de Paris was located, I yawned several times and found my eyelids getting that heavy feel. I'd had a good night's sleep, even if I had dreamed of appearing on *The Tonight Show* dressed as the Phantom Lady, so this sleepiness was a puzzle. I turned the stereo up a little louder and began to sing along, to wake myself up a bit.

I'd let Cicely pick the eatery, and that may have been a mistake. Beau Jardin de Paris was upscale and pricey, and while I don't mind a good meal out every now and then, I don't like to just open up the wallet and let the money fly out, which is what I felt like happened the only other time I'd been to this place. Overpriced, small portions. What's up with that? Just because the waitstaff puts on fancy clothes and they have a maître d' and cover all their food in a rich sauce doesn't mean they have to price the items as if they were succulent morsels of gold. And the name? It had been a while since my one French class (I dropped it, as I can barely speak English at seven thirty in the morning, let alone a foreign language), but Beau Jardin de Paris either meant Beautiful Gardens of Paris or I'm Dating a Guy Named Jardin in Paris. And honestly, even if it's the beautiful gardens one, it makes it sound like you're going to be chomping on rosebushes and grass.

The parking lot was fairly full, but I found a spot off to the side of the restaurant. Strangely, I seemed to zone out and was sitting in the car just staring ahead of me for several moments after shutting off the engine. Again, odd. I shook myself out of my reverie and went inside.

Ever notice how they keep French restaurants pretty dark inside? It's so you can't see what small portions they're giving you. It also explains why they use so much garlic—so you can find the food on your plate by smell. I was greeted by a middle-aged dude in a penguin suit.

"Does monsieur have a reservation?"

I blinked. His French accent was so affected, I thought for a moment he was imitating Peter Sellers in *The Pink Panther*. I almost struck a karate stance and yelled out, "Kato?" but I stopped myself in time. Penguin dude didn't look like he'd appreciate the joke even if he got the reference. "Yes, monsieur has. Name is Weasley."

He checked his book. "Ah, yes. Table for two."

"Yes, mademoiselle will be joining me shortly."

Smiling, he said, "Certainly, sir." And then he signaled for a waiter to show me to the table. The waiter was a young guy, maybe my age, with dark hair, brown eyes, and a jovial face. My eyes strayed to his ass as he was leading me through to the table. Not as nice as Tony's, of course, but if I was single (which, if I didn't get my act together I may well soon be!) it would do in a pinch. I don't know if it was because I was enjoying the slight wiggle of his derriere or because I just wasn't paying attention, but somehow along the way I stumbled over my own feet and had to grab hold of a nearby table to keep from falling flat on my face. Seated at the table were an older couple who were, understandably, somewhat put off by some young whippersnapper suddenly clutching their table with glasses and cutlery-shaking force.

"Sorry," I muttered before traipsing off after my waiter.

I heard the woman mutter to her companion, "He's drunk!"

Hubby agreed. "Stewed to the gills."

I frowned, but not because they were incorrect. In fact, I was feeling decidedly weird. Groggy. Clumsy. The waiter with the jiggly ass pulled out a chair for me, and I had to lower myself into it slowly to ensure I didn't slide across the damned thing and end up on the floor. What was wrong with me? Even my tongue felt funny. Thick and gummy.

"Would you like me to get you something while you are waiting?" Waiter guy asked.

"No, tank you," I said. Realizing what I'd said, I tried again. "Thank. No, thank you."

With a smile, he informed me his name was Dennis and he'd be happy to supply me with anything I needed. I almost asked him for a new, more alert brain and a tongue that didn't feel like it was coated in fur.

Moments later, Cicely sailed in. Actually, I didn't see the sailing, as she'd already pulled into port and had been deposited opposite me by Dennis before I'd even noticed. It was like a magic act. One minute, empty chair. The next it was occupied by Cicely. I blinked, wondering if illusionist Criss Angel was lurking in the wings. I looked at Cicely, who was gushing and settling into her seat and gazing at me with adoring eyes. She was speaking, but I started looking around at other tables, wondering if others were suddenly having people appear before them. No one else seemed to be having trouble with teleporting females. Had I zoned out again?

"You look," Cicely said, "very nice tonight."

"Thank you," I said, getting the word right this time. Was my head nodding, though? Why was it doing that? I thought about telling her she looked nice as well but nixed the idea. I was there to tell her I was gay and always would be, and that even if I wasn't I wouldn't be interested in her. Harsh, but it had to be done. Of course, I'd done it many times previously, and it hadn't seemed to stick in her head, but I was going to be blunt and direct this time. So no compliments. I had to remain firm.

Dennis came with menus, and we ordered. Everything was in French, but for my main course I ordered what I thought was some sort of chicken. Coq au vin. Maybe it was cock with wine? I just hoped it was the right kind of coq.

After Dennis shuffled off, Cicely began speaking. I had wanted to get right to the important stuff, namely that we could be friends, and I would visit her in the asylum once society realized she was a danger to man but that we could never be more than that, but I didn't get a chance. "What a day I've had!" she exclaimed. "I had to move up my hair appointment this morning, and my hairdresser, Jean-Claude, said that—"

I tried to focus on Jean-Claude's words of wisdom, but it was difficult. Cicely is a loud speaker, which you often find in these diminutive types, and her voice had a tone similar to the squeak of nails against a chalkboard, but somehow I found it hard to concentrate. I fought to keep my brain sharp. This was a tricky female, I reminded myself. She'd once had me agree to marry her, and I had been nearly unconscious at the time. I had to make sure no such pitfalls were awaiting me.

My eyelids continued to droop, and Cicely's speech began to sound like she was sitting several tables away. Suddenly I heard someone snort, and I sat up, almost alert. Cicely was saying something about her uncle, and how he and my stepfather had been playing golf last summer and something about them confusing the balls. She paused. I thought she'd come to the end of a funny story, so I chuckled. She stared at me. Apparently she hadn't got to the punch line yet.

"Did you just snort?" she asked me.

"Someone did. I think it was the guy behind me."

It hadn't been, of course. I'd snorted myself awake. I'd actually been falling asleep, sitting at a table, listening to Cicely screech on and on about golf balls.

"You look tired. I thought maybe it had been you and you were bored with my story."

"Oh, no," I assured her, although I meant, "Damn right!" And while I wanted to be firm with her, I didn't want to be unduly rude, so I added, "Go on. You were at the part where your uncle and my stepfather were brushing dust off each other's balls."

Rat Bastard

"So, anyway… why are you laughing?"

My words had caused a delayed reaction. "Just thinking about the stepmonster fondling some old dude's testicles. Funny thought."

Cicely peered at me hard. "There was nothing about testicles. I didn't say anything about testicles."

"No, but… balls. Testicles."

"I don't get it."

"No? Seemed funny to me." She could be right, though. For some reason I was in that beyond-tired state, when the smallest thing seems absolutely hysterical. "Go ahead with your story. I'm all ears."

"Well, they finally sorted out the ball thing—"

I stifled a smirk.

"—and Mr. Dollings teed up his ball. He was taking a few practice swings, when all of a sudden…."

I felt like I was being enveloped in a warm, comfy blanket. Maybe, I thought, if I closed my eyes for just a second, I could shake this tired feeling. I closed them.

Snork!

I jerked upright in my chair, eyes bulging. "What the hell was that?"

"That was you, my dear," Cicely said, a sympathetic look on her face. "Your stepfather told me that you'd started a job. Maybe you're overdoing things a bit. You really do look tired, and I'm afraid you dozed off for a moment there."

Did I? The snort certainly seemed to have come from my nasal passages. "I'm sorry. I can't think what's come over me." I bit my lip, not gently, and the pain seemed to wake me up a little. "Pray continue."

She smiled and reached over and touched my hand. "I love it when you talk Victorian, although you really should read something other than mysteries. I should pick a few authors for you to check out."

"Sounds"—hideous—"fantastic."

Just then, Dennis the waiter brought drinks. "Bon appétit," he said before departing again.

"I knew he was going to say that," I said. Were my words slurring? A familiar sound came from my hip pocket. My cell phone had a text message. Normally I would have ignored it, but I needed an excuse to extricate my hand from Cicely's. "Excuse me. This could be important."

It was from Jake. It read: *You okay? Because we may have, with the best of intentions, put something in your drink.*

"I was right," I said to Cicely. "It's important."

I texted back. *What???*

His reply came back fairly quick. *Thought you needed an excuse not to go, so crushed up sleeping tablets. Just a few. Four, I think. Okay, maybe five. Not more than that. Probably.*

I knew I was tired because I didn't scream aloud. I typed as fast as my lethargic fingers would allow. *You mixed alcohol and sleeping pills???? You ass!!!!* And then, just for emphasis, I added another exclamation point.

"Is everything all right?" Cicely asked, obviously concerned.

"Not sure, but I think I have to kill my best friend." My phone bleeped to let me know a new message had arrived. *There was no alcohol in that drink! Just blue food coloring, grapefruit juice, pomegranate juice, orange juice, and a few bits of stuff we found in the fridge! And the sleeping pills, of course.*

Oh, good. I wasn't going to die. Just go into a coma. I typed. *You dastard! What about my date with Tony????* It was supposed to be bastard, but I hit the wrong key. The point, I think, was made, though.

The reply: *Didn't know about date with Tony at the time. My bad.*

I set the phone on the table, making a mental note to smack my friend soundly the next time I saw him. At least now I knew why I felt so strange. Morpheus, that Greek dream dude, was hovering over one shoulder, while the sandman was hovering over the other, sprinkling me with his sleep dust.

"What is it?" Cicely asked. "You look like you just got bad news."

I did, but telling her wouldn't change anything. She'd just gush over me, and I was too groggy to fight her off. Best to just dig down deep and force myself to stay awake. Now that I knew that, for all intents and purposes, I'd been drugged, surely my mind could combat the effects of the sleeping pills. And I had a mission to accomplish.

I gave Cicely my best "sorry" face. "We need to talk."

"We are talking."

"About something specific. You seem to think, if you persist enough, that at some point I'll suddenly become heterosex—"

Dennis chose that moment to return, placing bowls of soup before us. Soup! That should buck me up a little! As Dennis started to walk away, I shoved a spoonful into my mouth. And what the hell! "Dennis!" I called.

Our waiter returned. "Yes, sir?"

"This soup is cold."

"It's vichyssoise, sir. It's supposed to be cold."

"You mean the kitchen just opens up a can and dumps it into a bowl and they charge you five bucks for it?"

The waiter gave me an indulgent smile. "I assure you, sir, that the chef makes—"

"I was joking, Dennis. You'll have to forgive me. I'm not feeling my best right now." In fact, the room, already dim, was becoming dimmer, mainly due to my eyelids closing. Dennis, now satisfied I was completely bonkers, left us to enjoy our cold soup. I tried it again. Potato-ey. Might be good if it was at least warm, the way soups were meant to be.

Cicely smiled at me. Everyone seemed to be smiling at me. Even people at adjoining tables. "So, you were saying?"

"Cicely, I'm sure you're a very nice person when you're not madly stalking some poor guy, but I've got to tell you that you're barking up the wrong tree. I'm gay. I'm always going to be gay. It's not a phase. It's who and what I am."

At least, that was the speech I intended to say. I don't know how much of it came mumbling out of my mouth. I was vaguely aware of my eyes closing and hearing a splashing sound, which I later realized was my face literally doing a nosedive into the vichyssoise. The last thing I heard was Cicely screaming and myself going, "Glug!"

Chapter Twelve

THE ADVERTISING gurus behind the campaign for the brand of sleeping tablets Jake used to dope me promised that "You'll wake refreshed!" I didn't. I awoke feeling like a hedgehog had just crawled out of my mouth, and my head felt like Michael Jordan had been using it to practice his jump shots. It was too much effort to open both eyes at once, so I started with the left one.

I expected to wake up in a hospital room with doctors and nurses hovering around the bed, saying they barely saved my life. Strangely, I seemed to be in my room at the Phantom Lady. I took stock.

I wasn't dead.

I wasn't in the hospital.

It was morning. (I could see the sunlight streaming into the window.)

I was still dressed, although someone had removed my shoes.

Cicely was sitting in a chair next to my bed, looking worried.

When I lifted my hand to rub my face, it felt like I was moving an appendage that belonged to someone else. The hand, not working properly yet, just sort of brushed along the side of my face, the fingers saying, "Fuck this shit, we're on strike." The result was that I kind of smacked myself in the face more than rubbed life into my cheeks, but it did wake me up enough to make me realize that it was indeed Cicely sitting bedside and not some hallucination.

"Um," I said. "Hello."

"You're awake!"

I thought, as I was speaking and moving appendages about, that this was obvious. "Yes," was all I said though.

"We were so worried about you!" Cicely reached over and grasped my hand. Grasped it pretty hard, to be honest. The pain was good, though. It forced the rest of the sleepiness out of me and brought all the feeling back to the extremities.

"That's nice," I said. "Um… what happened?"

"You fell asleep in your soup."

"That much I sort of remember."

Cicely smiled at me. It was the kind of smile you use on an infant who just went "goo" for the first time or on a puppy that has finally mastered paper training. "The restaurant wanted to call an ambulance, but I convinced them that you were only tired."

"Well, true. But why—"

"I hope you don't mind, but I read your phone messages."

I frowned. "I don't—"

"Your phone was still out, and I thought at first that you had read something that made you faint. When you were getting those texts, you looked, to put it bluntly, sick." She squeezed my hand a little more. It was meant to be an encouraging squeeze, but it was a crusher. For a little gal, Cicely has a grip on her. "There was a lot of shouting and commotion after you collapsed, and while they were pulling you out of the soup and feeling for a pulse, I grabbed your phone. I looked at your messages and saw what had happened. It was a very stupid thing for your friend to do."

"We agree on that."

"I smacked him when I saw him."

I bet Jake had one hell of a bruise to show for it. "The least he deserves."

"Anyway, I knew you'd been drugged with sleeping pills. I figured you didn't really need a trip to the hospital. After all, it was only a few pills, and even then, as I learned from your friend later, you only had a few sips. And I wasn't sure how it would look if it got out that you'd been given a laced drink. I'm not sure, but it sounds illegal."

Legalities had never stopped Jake before. "How did I get here?" I asked.

"Well, after telling the restaurant staff that you suffered from narcolepsy—"

"Swift thinking," I said. Credit where credit is due. Cicely may be borderline insane and a stalker of the first order, but she was a *smart* loony and stalker.

"Thank you. Anyway, I used your phone and called your friend, Jake. I figured, since he was responsible for your condition, that he should help me get you home." She looked about the room. "I didn't know you were living here. I thought you still had an apartment in Rockford."

"Working here, it's just easier to live here as well. The room is small, but it suits my needs."

Cicely frowned. "I must say, your phone was a font of information."

"You went through my messages?" I was slightly alarmed. There were some juicy texts between Tony and me. On the other hand, I had to get her to see she had no chance with me, so maybe it was a good thing she read them.

"Yes, first there was Jake's statement that he thought you needed an excuse to get out of our date."

"To be honest, at first I was reluctant to see you, but I wanted to set the record straight between us, so—"

She seemed not to hear me. "And then there were all those messages from some guy named Tony." She eyed me with suspicion. "Quite a lot of them."

"He's my boyfriend, or at least will be if we can ever get together."

"Boyfriend." She said the word flatly.

"Yes, boyfriend. You knew I was gay. Always have been, always will be."

Cicely shook her head. "I don't really believe you are. You're just confused."

"You should have seen me in women's underwear, traipsing through the snow and shinnying up trees." I sighed. It was a deep one. I hated breaking anyone's heart, even one belonging to a deluded, mushy female. "Cicely, I'm gay. You know this. I'm not confused, or in a phase, or anything else. I sleep with men. I have a boyfriend. You've met him. His name is Tony. You met him at Winston Manor once, and at the time you seemed to have understood that I was with him and that I'd never be with you. You ran off crying, if I remember correctly."

The incident of which I speak was actually a fairly recent event on the calendar. It had been when I'd met Tony during a stay at Jake's family estate (if people in northern Illinois can actually have estates, otherwise we'll just call it a big-ass house) just months previously. The sight of Cicely, after giving my face a good slap, storming out of the library with angry tears running down her cheeks was seared on my memory. It wasn't, it seemed, seared on hers.

"I was," she admitted, "a little miffed at you that night. But now I see that your infatuation with that young man is only due to your trepidation over commitment. You know, deep down, that we're soul mates, and you're not willing to give up your freedom just yet, so you have this whole sexual confusion thing going on."

"Again, not confused. Gay. How can I get through to you? Penis good. Vagina yucky."

"Speaking of that boy, he was here earlier."

I sat up quickly, suddenly more awake than I'd been in my entire life. "What? Tony was here?"

"Yes, he stopped in a few hours ago. He seemed to wonder what I was doing in your room. I told him that your fiancée had every right to be in your bedroom."

Rat Bastard

If I could have jumped in shock while sitting up in a bed, I would have. "What? What do you mean, fiancée?"

"You and me. We're getting married."

"Since when?"

"You asked me to marry you that weekend at Winston Manor."

I hadn't, actually, but there was no telling Cicely that. "But… you broke that off!"

"No, I didn't."

"You slapped me in the face and told me it was over. That's pretty much breaking it off, in my book."

She shrugged. "Just a lover's tiff. I've forgiven you since then."

I quickly swung my legs around and rose from the bed—on the opposite side from where Cicely was sitting. I wanted to keep some distance between us. It was time for no-nonsense, simple language even a loony could understand. "Cicely, we're not getting married."

"Yes, dear, we are."

"No, we're not. For one thing, when the preacher got to the point where he asks if there's anyone present that knows of any reason why the two of us should not be bound in holy wedlock, I know of several guys who'd jump up and say 'I do! He likes cock!' But the main thing is that I don't love you. I never will. I'm gay. I think I love Tony. And I hope he loves me. Or at least that we have a chance together, if you haven't blown it by telling him that we're getting married." I was looking around the room desperately. "Where's my phone?"

Cicely watched as I patted down my pockets and searched the top of my dresser, shoving aside pictures, loose change, and my car keys trying to find the damned thing. Finally she said, "I think I still have it. Let me check."

I waited, almost hopping from one leg to the other while she rummaged through her handbag, which she'd placed at the foot of her chair. Eventually she fished out my phone. "I guess I must have kept hold of it after you'd done your swan dive into the soup."

She gave it to me, and I punched buttons. With each ring, my heart sank even farther. *Pick up,* I prayed, *please pick up.* More rings, and then I got his voice mail. "Tony, call me as soon as you can. All can be explained."

Cicely made a face. "I don't know why you're getting so worked up."

"He's my boyfriend, or I want him to be! And he comes here to see me and finds you in my bedroom!"

"I'm your fiancée. I'm sure he understands."

"You're not my fiancée! Do you really want a fiancé who has a boyfriend? Don't you see, somewhere in that fuzzy mind of yours, that the two things don't go together?"

Her lip trembled, and tears looked imminent. "Are you saying," she said, voice a-quiver, "that you don't want to marry me?"

"Yes! That's what I'm saying! You wouldn't be happy with me! Believe me! For one thing, we'd never have sex, and—"

"Of course we would. That's what married people do."

"Don't tell my Uncle Phil and my Aunt Jane that." I paced a bit, thinking hard. Maybe Tony wasn't upset over finding Cicely bedside. After all, it wasn't like he hadn't met her. He knew she was my personal stalker and that she didn't seem to listen to the voice of reason when it came to yours truly. On the other hand, he hadn't stuck around or left a note. Why didn't he call back?

"So, you're calling off the engagement?" Cicely was staring straight ahead, obviously distressed. I felt sorry for her, but what could I do? I had to get through to her once and for all.

"In a nutshell, yes. Although, I really should point out that there never really was an engagement and that it was all in your head. Tough to hear, I know, but sometimes the truth isn't pleasant."

She nodded. "I guess, then, that I'll have to tell your stepfather that I won't be publishing my book with his firm."

Panic began to well up in me, but just for a moment. The idea of what my stepmonster's reaction would be filled my heart with dread. But then I thought *so what? So he blows a gasket. What can he do to me?* I had enough money to get Tony's ring. I was working, making money. True, he could cut off my allowance and refuse to pay for next year's tuition—I never did get him to sign an agreement, dammit!—but I could save for that. I'd lose the Corvette, possibly, and that wrenched my guts, but it would be a small price to pay if I could finally rid myself of the albatross known as Cicely Talbot.

"I guess you should," I said.

She looked up sharply. "What?"

"I said you should tell him, if you feel strongly about it. It won't change my mind."

"He'll be very cross," she said, her eyes narrowing.

"He wakes up very cross and progresses to downright miffed by lunchtime before settling into full-on anger by evening. I've gotten used to it."

My attitude seemed to stymie her. "He'll cut you off. You won't have any money."

I shrugged. "I guess I won't." And then her words sank in. "My stepfather has talked to you about me?"

"You've come up in conversation, of course."

"And he's suggested to you that you should keep pursuing me," I said.

"He thinks you should be married, if that's what you mean. And he thinks I'd be a good wife for you."

The bastard! He was fueling the poor girl's infatuation with me, not only to get her to publish with his firm but to marry me off. To a woman, yet. "But he knows I'm gay."

"He feels the same way I do, that it's a sort of protestation. An act of rebellion."

"I've been doing a heck of a lot of protesting and rebelling since I turned sixteen, then." I glanced at the clock on the wall. "I'm glad we had this chat and were able to set the record straight. Sorry and all that, but you'll have to find another devilishly handsome, skinny guy to pine after. I hear they have a lot of them in Des Moines. You should try there. But right now I've got to take a shower and get ready for work. So you'd better be heading back to Rockford."

She stood, picking up her handbag. "Oh, I don't have to go anywhere. I've booked a room here."

"You can't have. We're full up."

"There was a cancellation, so I snapped it up. Besides, your stepfather has that Christmas party here on Wednesday. I was going to stay here a day or two anyway. Who knows," she said as she moved slowly to the door, "I might just get a chance to see the Phantom Lady."

"Look close. She could be nearer than you think."

I let her puzzle over that. Finally getting her out of the room, I once again tried to reach Tony. No luck. By the time I'd showered and changed clothes and gone down to man the front desk, I'd left ten more messages in his voice mail. With each one my worry grew. What if he'd grown tired of our lack of contact, and coming and finding Cicely watching over my sleeping body had been the final straw?

My brow was furrowed, and I wasn't at my chirpiest as I began my shift. While the phone wasn't as active as it had been just after the ghost sighting, I still had to field quite a few calls. There were more bookings, mostly for the weekend, and I even managed to arrange a New Year's party for an insurance company. I was still busy on the phone when, out of the corner of my eye, I saw a large shape looming up to the desk. I figured it was just one of the guests who'd forgotten their key or something, so I finished the call quickly and looked up, slapping a smile in place. "Can I help you—"

That's as far as I got. Standing before me, smiling an evil smile if I ever had seen one, was Gates Stumpenhorst. "I'd like a room, please."

Rat Bastard

"Sorry," I said, the voice only slightly squeaky with fear. The desk was pretty sturdy, and I was glad it was between him and me, but he was a strong dude, and I feared that one or two pounds against the counter by those meat hooks he referred to as hands would send the whole thing splintering to pieces, leaving me defenseless. "We're all booked up."

"Are you sure?" he asked, stepping even closer. He was wearing a coat, and the thickness of the garment made him seem even more threatening. Chuck Norris would no doubt quiver a little seeing this Stumpenhorst flex his biceps. "I'm quite determined to stay here. I've got unfinished business to attend to."

I swallowed hard. "Pretty sure." I looked down at the signing-in book for the merest of seconds and then looked up again. "Yep. Not a room to be had."

Mr. Rivers chose that moment to appear, coming down the stairs. He smiled as he came closer and held up a finger to get my attention. "Oh, Wombat. Glad you're here. The Johnsons, who were staying in Room Five, have had to leave suddenly. Mel is making it up right now, so that room is free for the next few days. I'm sure we won't have any trouble renting it." Beaming, he passed us and headed toward the dining room.

Stumpenhorst stared at me. "I'd like Room Five, please."

"It's not a very nice room. I don't think you'll like it. Drafty. And the bed is short. Your feet will dangle over the edge."

"I'll take Room Five," Stumpenhorst repeated through clenched teeth.

"They have very nice rooms at the motel in town."

"Room Five has everything I need." It was amazing how chilling Stumpenhorst could make his voice without actually doing much. Just an even tone, but with an edge to it. Movie villains have this down to a tee. Alan Rickman, I believe, teaches classes on the subject.

"Really? Can't imagine what Room Five has that would entice anyone to fork out dough to spend a night there."

Stumpenhorst leaned forward, bringing his face close to mine. "Proximity. It has proximity to someone I'm going to beat the snot out of. And now, I'll have plenty of chances."

I must admit, the hands shook a bit as I completed his transaction. Visions of myself pounded to a pulp kept coming into my head, and it's hard to concentrate on much else when the mind is running newsreel footage of a bloody beating. I handed Stumpenhorst his key. "There you are, sir," I said. Mr. Rivers also liked for us to add "Enjoy your stay with us," but I couldn't bring myself to speak the words. I knew what Stumpenhorst would consider an enjoyable time, and the thought sent shivers down the spine.

Palming the key in his meaty hand, Stumpenhorst smiled one of those smiles tigers favor at feeding time. "What time do you get off work?"

"Seven." It was actually six, but Stumpenhorst didn't need to know that I wanted an hour to find a good hiding place.

"I'll be waiting," he said, and then he tramped off. And if someone can tramp off ominously, Stumpenhorst did it as if he'd mastered ominous tramping off.

Chapter Thirteen

I WAS thinking the day could hardly get worse, but fate had it in for guys nicknamed Weasel that day. I tried, during lulls, to reach Tony several more times, still with no success. I was sinking into despair when, finally, I got a text from him. It simply read *We'll talk later.* I was formulating a reply when the front door opened and in walked Deputy Bradley. He didn't look happy.

He stamped the snow off his boots and then approached. "We had another fire last night," he said, eyes narrowed with suspicion.

"Did you?" I asked.

He nodded. "Someone set fire to the Dumpster behind the filling station on Gentry Street."

"Seems a bit mean," I said, "torching an innocent Dumpster."

"Firebugs don't stop there, though," the deputy said, shaking his head sadly. "They start off setting fire to Dumpsters, but then they can't stop themselves. It's buildings next. They start off with small ones, sheds, garages, but then go on to houses, businesses." He eyed me steadily. "Were you working last night?"

It was nice to be able to smile. "I have an alibi for last night. I was with a girl all night. Cicely Talbot. She's staying here. You can ask her."

"And what time did you meet up with this girl?"

"I met her at Beau Jardin de Paris at seven." I added, as the good deputy seemed confused, "That's a French restaurant."

He nodded. "The fire," he said, "was probably set shortly before seven. You could have left here, started your little conflagration, and then gone to meet the young lady."

"I could have, but didn't. I'm not your firebug. Honest."

The nodding continued. "I'm not saying you are. Just said you *could* have done it. Still keeping my eye on you." He added some narrowing of the eyes to go with the nodding. I suspect they teach narrowing of the eyes the first day at Cop School, or maybe they just all think it makes them look like Clint Eastwood. Bradley didn't look like Clint Eastwood. More a Kathy Bates with less chest and a mustache. "Have I told you we have a description?"

"You haven't mentioned it."

"Eyewitness. Says the arsonist is tall."

"Well, that must narrow the search down a bit."

"And blond."

I could see where this was going. "Still—"

"And thin."

"Has basketball legend Larry Bird been in the area, making personal appearances?"

That flummoxed him. "What?"

"Larry Bird. Basketball player of yesteryear. Tall, thin, blond. Fits the description perfectly. I'd cuff him as soon as he's spotted again. Although it's been years since I've seen a picture of him. He might have gray hair now. It's been a while since he played. I have to admit I haven't kept up with his career."

Bradley frowned. "Larry Bird isn't a suspect!"

"Ah. Crossed him off the list, eh? Iron clad alibi, I suppose. Still, not the only tall, thin blond running around. Last time I was at the Twenty-One Club, there was a whole gaggle of them. You'd have thought someone was cloning them."

The deputy made a sound that I believe is normally spelled pshaw. And he pshawed with emphasis. "Just keep your nose clean," he growled.

He left after that, and for once I wasn't annoyed that a deceived deputy suspected me of arson. If Bradley was keeping an eye on me, maybe that was a good thing. He might just be nearby when Stumpenhorst pounced, and it wouldn't be a bad thing to have a dude handy with a gun when that happened. Stumpenhorst might have resembled a charging rhino, but even charging rhinos think twice when confronted with a gun. Well, the discerning charging rhinos do.

Nearing the end of my shift, I began to get a little antsy. And who could blame me? I had a Stumpenhorst on the premises who wanted to rearrange the nose on my face, not to mention my own personal stalker in residence. My plan, as soon as the proverbial whistle blew, indicating my work was through for the day, was to bolt up the stairs to my room and lock the door behind me. I'd get hold of Tony and we could talk and hopefully I could explain everything to his satisfaction.

At the stroke of six, my replacement—in the form of a grinning Austin—barely in place, I shot out from behind the desk and ran up the stairs as fast as my long legs would take me, nearly colliding with Mrs. Kendall and her dog. Apologizing and pausing just long enough to give Rodney the Dog a scritch between the ears, I continued on.

My haste was warranted, for once I'd reached the first floor landing, I heard a door opening. Out of the corner of my eye, I saw it was Room Five, and a hulking figure was emerging. I picked up the pace, hearing a satisfied "Aha!" behind me. I had too much of a head start, however, and with Stumpenhorst's plodding feet sounding on the stairs, I reached my room and threw myself in and locked the door behind me. Seconds later there was the trump-trump of his footsteps as they got to my door. The idiot tried the knob, only to find it wouldn't budge. He then pounded on the door. "Come out of there!"

"Have you thought this through?" I asked. "I mean, why ask me to willingly go out there and get pummeled? On my list of things to do today, getting beaten up wasn't one of the items."

Again he hammered against the wood. Then the wood groaned in protest and the entire doorframe shook. The hulk must have put his shoulder to it in an attempt to break in. "Come out of there!"

"If you break that door," I said, pretty reasonably I thought, "you'll have to pay for it."

That put a pause to the door abuse. After a short silence, Stumpenhorst said, "I just want to talk with you."

"Talk. I like to have a few inches of wood in between me and some speakers. I can hear you just fine."

He rattled the doorknob again, hoping, no doubt, that magically it was now unlocked. It wasn't.

"Come out here and talk."

"Busy, thanks."

I could almost sense him seething out in the hall. His words sounded like they were coming through clenched teeth. "I'm going to pound the fuck out of you when I get hold of you! Now come out of there!"

"Those two sentences don't go together. Just to let you know."

Again he knocked against the door with his oversized fists. "I'm going to kill you!"

"Listen," I said.

"I don't want to listen. I want to beat the snot out of you!"

"Well, listen for now. You might learn something. Logical thinking. You want to beat me up because I'm dating your ex." Well, I *hoped* I was still dating Tony. "Say you do get hold of me and smack me around. What then? Will Tony say to himself, 'Wow. What a man. I broke up with him and he went and pounded the guy I'm now dating. I want him back!' Or will he say, 'What an ass. I'm going to tend to my new boyfriend's wounds and tell this ape Stumpenhorst where to get off.' Which do you think will happen?"

There was a short silence as the brute mulled this over. "I guess he wouldn't like it."

"You bet he wouldn't. Now, why don't you be a nice primate and go off and find a tree to climb?"

This met with a short pause, followed by the rattling of the doorknob. "Come out of there!"

"Haven't you been paying attention? Tony won't be yours if you pummel me. It doesn't work that way."

"Yeah, but I just want to pound the shit out of you!"

"Why?"

"Because you're an asshole, and you annoy me when you constantly talk shit! You prattle like... well, I don't know what! But it just makes me want to punch you!"

Fair dues. And one should give him snaps for using the word prattle. I wouldn't have thought they would have bothered much with vocabulary when teaching the young Stumpenhorst, thinking, quite rightly, that there was a limited amount of working space in his skull and they shouldn't overdo things.

I turned on the television, more to drown him out than for entertainment. Eventually, I knew, he would tire of lurking in the hallway and slither off to his own room or to get some grub or to visit a local bar and pick a fight with some drunk. His fists, it was obvious, were itching and needed a workout. I just wanted to make sure they didn't get hitting practice with my face as the target.

I decided to play some video games while waiting for Stumpenhorst to tire. I pulled a chair up closer to the television for optimum playing and was soon immersed in trying to get my half-vampire character through a village that obviously had some prejudice against half vampires. Every now and then, I'd hear a thump on the door or the rattle of the knob, but I ignored them. Stumpenhorst even tried the old Pretend To Walk Away But Really Not Go Anywhere trick, but it was a clumsy attempt. Finally, he tired.

"You can't hide in there forever," he growled.

"You underestimate my sense of self-preservation."

"I'll find you sometime, you know." And with that, he really did leave.

To be honest, I was hardly concentrating on the game. I think I'd talked to everyone in the virtual village at least twice and hadn't paid any attention to their conversation, adding nothing to my knowledge of the whereabouts of the treasure my character was seeking. I was just leaving the village when a passing troll, who bore more than a superficial resemblance to Stumpenhorst, leaped out from behind a tree, brandishing a sword and making some threatening gestures at my half vampire. It may have been only a video game, but the sight made my heart race, and I nearly caused the chair I was sitting in to fall backward when I nearly leaped out of my skin. I shut off the game. I needed calm, and Stumpenhorsts and trolls weren't providing it.

To illustrate just how nervous I was, when I stood to turn the television and game console off and my cell phone buzzed, I nearly hit the ceiling and lost control of my bowels. Luckily for the top of my head and my self-esteem, neither of these actually happened, but I feel it was a close call. Telling my heart to calm down a bit and attempt to beat normally, I answered the call. It was Tony.

"Hey," he said. "I know this phone is new, but you don't have to fill it right away. After I finished working, I looked, and I think I've got seventeen text messages from you, and my voice mail is literally full of you telling me to call you."

He didn't sound upset, which was a great relief. I immediately went from worried to ecstatically happy. I sat on the edge of my bed, my legs not feeling up to the task of keeping me standing. "I thought you were mad at me," I said.

"Why would you think that, just because I came to see you and I found a girl administering to your needs who told me that she was your fiancée?"

"That would be the reason, yes. You're not upset?"

I heard him sigh. "I was a little miffed at first, I have to admit. I mean, you've told me about Cicely, and the one time I'd met her previously I have to admit she struck me as pretty strange, but it just seems to me that you've put up with her enough. Talk to her, tell her in no uncertain terms that you're gay—"

"I've done this. Numerous times. She thinks it's a phase."

Tony made a noise. Kind of an annoyed chuckle. "Well, after I thought about it, I wasn't so mad at you. You've told me she's stalked you for years now."

"Since a Christmas party my mother gave. Cicely seemed to think mistletoe actually had magical properties and the mere fact that, at one point, purely by accident, we both were standing beneath the damned thing meant something. She's been a barnacle on the good ship Weasel ever since."

"You've got to get rid of her. Get a restraining order or something."

"I think I've finally convinced her that she'll never have me. Tough on her, of course, but it had to be done. Earlier, I finally chiseled my way into her brain and made her see sense. Sorry, by the way, that I missed our date last night. Slept through it, it seems."

"Yeah, your friend Jake told me that he put some sleeping pills in your drink."

"He didn't know I was supposed to see you later. Doesn't mean he's not an idiot and shouldn't be locked away so that he can't give diphenhydramine-laced drinks to people."

"I take it that's what's in sleeping pills." Tony laughed. "You have the strangest brain, full of arcane things."

"Know thy enemy. Plus I looked up what he gave me on the Internet earlier. I like to know what's trying to kill me." I made a face and then realized I was talking on the phone and was wasting a good facial expression. "Speaking of things trying to kill me, I had a narrow escape mere hours ago. Your ex, one Gates Stumpenhorst, showed a desire to pound me into guacamole."

"Gates? What's he doing there?"

I filled Tony in on the recent events involving Stumpenhorst, leaving out no detail. When I finished, I heard Tony sigh heavily.

Stephen Osborne

"It's partially my fault. I had only just recently broken up with him when I met you, and, although I told him there was no one else, he suspected I left him for someone else, someone who, in his mind, came between us."

"Came between you and me?"

"No, me and Gates."

"Ah, I see. So then when he took a gander at me at the fast food joint, he naturally thought I was the one who split you two asunder."

"Exactly."

"Sucks to be him. The guy always seems to be wrong, doesn't have you anymore, and has ears that stick out like saucers. Can't be pleasant."

"Still, I don't want him beating you up."

"Oh, I can take care of myself," I said with more courage than I felt.

"Well, I might be able to get away later. There's a big dinner party here, but it shows signs of breaking up early. If it does, and I can get everything cleaned up in time, I'll drive down there and we can spend some time together. Hopefully I can talk to Gates too, and get him to see reason."

"That would be nice."

The chatting was cut short then as Tony was called back to his duties at Winston Manor. We hung up after Tony reiterated that he hoped he'd see me later.

After the call, I was in much better spirits, although I still was wary of leaving my room, as there might be a Stumpenhorst lurking in the shadows. I decided to rejoin Holmes on my Kindle and while away the time reading a Doyle story or two while I waited to see if Tony would be able to make it. I walked over to my nightstand to get the device and nearly tripped over a paper bag sitting next to my bed. At first, I couldn't imagine what a paper bag was doing there, but then I recalled that after my stint as the Phantom Lady I'd stuffed Sammy's wig and the women's underwear into said bag with the intent to give the stuff back to the cook at my earliest convenience. I picked up the sack and deposited it onto the bed, intending to shove it into the closet later to await a time when I could return the stuff to the proper owners. I then grabbed my Kindle and went to sit down and see what Holmes and Watson were up to.

Ever notice how, just as you get settled into a comfy chair armed with reading material that the bladder suddenly decides it's allowed you enough free time and wants to be relieved? I had barely gotten into the story when I knew I couldn't wait until a good stopping point. I had to hit the bathroom, and fairly quickly, or I was going to get a warm trickle down my leg. The question was, was it safe? Would I open my door only to find a Stumpenhorst there, ready to spring and say, "Aha!"? It would have been nice to have a private bathroom, but those rooms were for guests only. There was, I noted, a vase on my dresser with some plastic flowers in it, and I thought about using that and just forgetting chancing leaving the safety of my room, but second thoughts made it clear a vase might not be the best solution. For one, it wasn't a particularly large vase, and overfilling would be a disaster. But more to the point, having a vase full of pee in the room when Tony arrived wouldn't do. Nothing puts one off the idea of amore than the smell of urine, unless you're into that sort of thing. Which I wasn't.

I trod over to the door as quietly as possible and unlocked it, half expecting it to spring open with gale force to reveal a bevy of maddened Stumpenhorsts poised to trample me. Breathing a sigh of relief, I saw that the hallway was empty.

Creeping out on tiptoes, I got almost to the bathroom door when I heard a floorboard creak behind me. I started and whirled, and let me tell you doing both of those things simultaneously when you've got to take a piss in the worst way isn't recommended. Nothing actually leaked out, but only because I bit my lower lip to keep everything in check. My heart, which had been doing calisthenics, calmed down when it realized that the heavy tread it had heard belonged to Jake Winston and not Gates Stumpenhorst.

"There you are!" Jake said, a little too loudly for my liking. "I've been wondering if you were up and about."

"Keep it down!" I said with a clenched jaw. "Stumpenhorst may be close by, and he wants to kill me."

"What's a Stumpenhorst?"

I was having to hop from one foot to the other, and certain bodily functions were yelling at me, telling me this wasn't the time for chat. The bladder was demanding action, not inactivity. "I'll tell you, but it will have to be through the door," I said as I rushed into the lavatory.

I could tell Jake was pressed against the door to get the best acoustics to hear my words, which unfortunately also meant he heard a bit of splashing and the relieved moan that escaped my lips as the stream began to flow. "Wow. You really had to go."

"Yes. But to get back to the point, Gates Stumpenhorst is Tony's ex. The big dude we met outside of the restaurant that day."

"Oh, yeah. I remembered he had a weird name but forgot exactly what it was. He's here?"

"Obviously, otherwise—" I paused here for the obligatory tap-tap and flush. "—I wouldn't be worried about him beating me to a pulp."

"Your whole fan club must be here. I was just going to tell you that your stepfather checked in earlier. Maybe the two of them can get together and draw straws to see who gets to stomp you."

"Actually, I've got a bit of a detente going with the old stepmonster right now. Although that will probably end when he hears from Cicely Talbot. He was only putting up with me to get to her."

"What the hell are you doing now? Playing with it? Give it a rest, Weasel!"

"I'm washing my hands, doofus. And speaking of you being a doofus, what about that stunt with the sleeping pills?"

"Meant with the best of intentions, I assure you. I thought you'd down the whole drink right there and be too sleepy to even go out. Figured I'd have to carry you up to your room, and then I'd call Cicely and tell her that you suddenly came over all sick. You said you didn't want to go on the date."

"And so you thought you'd drug me? You're a menace to society."

"You might be right. Still, sorry how things turned out. If I'd known you had a date with Tony after…."

"Yes, well, from now on, let me get out of my dates on my own, thank you very much." Finished with my ablution, I opened the door. Jake had been leaning against it, and the sudden movement almost caused him to fall into the bathroom, but I steadied him. I looked beyond him to make sure the coast was clear. Seeing no Stumpenhorsts, I sighed with relief. "Now, if you'll excuse me, I'm going to hide in my room until Tony arrives."

"He's coming?"

"Hopefully. He thought he could get away from his duties and join me. And I hope he can. We're getting dangerously close to the final stages of the Boyfriend Zone. If we don't get something going soon, we're sunk."

"Well," Jake said, placing an encouraging hand on my shoulder, "I wish you well. I've got a date with Keith myself tonight. Luckily, we don't have to worry about the Boyfriend Zone. We've been rutting like rabbits in an Easter Parade."

I raised an eyebrow. "What Easter Parades have you been going to? Well, mixed metaphors aside, enjoy yourself."

We parted, and I rushed back to my room. The whole way down the hall, I expected Stumpenhorst to rear his ugly head, but I made it without incident and closed the door behind me with a sigh. I got settled back in my chair, powered up my reader, and got lost in the Victorian world of Conan Doyle for a while. Eventually, though, the eyelids began to droop. I looked at the clock on the wall and saw it was nearing the midnight hour. I did some mental calculations and figured, with finishing up with the dinner party and the drive from Winston Manor and adding a few minutes to primp, that Tony should be showing up shortly. I set aside Holmes and thought I'd pull the bedsheets down a bit and make everything look inviting. Not subtle, but I couldn't afford subtleties. I turned off all the lights but one as well, giving the room a hopefully romantic tone.

The paper bag containing wig and underwear was still on the bed. Not wanting Tony to think I was overly kinky and couldn't enjoy a good romp in the hay without dressing up like a woman, I took the bag to the closet. There was a nice spot for the bag at the back, behind my shoes and the bags containing my bowling ball and tennis rackets. I was bending over in the shadowy confines of the closet to place it there when I heard my doorknob jiggle.

I froze, bag still in hand. I had, in my haste coming back from the bathroom, forgotten to lock the door behind me. Chances were the handle jiggler was Tony, but what if it was Stumpenhorst? I thrust myself into the closet just to be safe. I pulled the door nearly closed, leaving just enough space for me to see into the room. If it was Tony, I could come out and explain. If it was Stumpenhorst, I was going to see if I could shrink into the corner and become nearly invisible and pray he wouldn't search the room.

I peered through the crack. It wasn't Tony or Stumpenhorst. It was Cicely. And she was wearing what I believe is termed a nightie. A white, filmy sort of thing, anyway. She looked around the room and saw it was empty. Instead of leaving, though, she got a weird sort of smile on her face and walked over to the bed. Seeing that I'd pulled down the covers must have been too much of a temptation for her. A quick movement, and the nightie, if that's what it was, was off and onto the floor, and a naked Cicely was standing there.

Chapter Fourteen

I'VE SEEN the naked female form before. Mostly in pictures, of course. Every now and then while growing up, one of my straight friends would show me a porno DVD, saying "Isn't this hot?" and I'd be thinking "Yes, but not in the way you think it is. Lose the women and you've got something here." And I have gay friends who are obsessed with female mammaries. I'm not one of them. To me, a boob is just a boob. A mound of flesh. You could show me a dozen, and I'd go, "Eh." Some are bigger. Some are firmer. If they danced and made sounds like maracas, that would be different. A coolness factor would be added, although they still wouldn't make my junk stand up and take notice.

Cicely's were small and firm. As boobs go, they were boobs. As for her nether regions.... Well, we won't go there. I, for one, certainly had no intention of going there. It seemed, though, that it *was* her intention that I'd go there, because she slipped her naked self into the bed and drew the covers up over her.

"The hell!"

Cicely sat up, perplexed, and her eyes went to the closet. I was a bit on the perplexed side myself, because I hadn't meant to say the words aloud. Although I can't really blame the old vocal chords. The sight of Cicely in the buff, slipping between my sheets, warranted an exclamation of some sort, and I thought they were behaving themselves admirably by keeping to a fairly tame cuss word such as hell.

"Patrick? Is that you?"

There was no point in pretending a voice hadn't come from the closet. "Yep. Me all right."

"What are you doing in the closet?"

"Oh, you know. This and that. More to the point, what are you doing sans clothing in my bed?"

She smiled. I think she meant it as a sweet smile, but Cruella De Vil would have shuddered upon seeing it. "I'm here to transform you."

"Exqueaze me?"

"Oh, you know. Make you see the light. Get you over this fixation you have that you're gay."

"I *am* gay. It's not a phase or a fixation. And I'm not having sex with you, so put that thing back on and get back to your own room."

Her lips did the pout thing. "Are you going to come out of there?"

"I'm fine here. Best option I have at the moment."

Finding pouting didn't work, she tried seduction. Sitting up farther, she let the bedsheets fall from her upper body, exposing once again her small but admittedly perky breasts. She cupped them in her hands, pointing them at me like they were dangerous weapons. Which, I suppose, they were. "Don't you want to fondle these?"

I did the only thing I could. I closed the closet door.

"Patrick! Come out of there!"

"No."

"Come out here and have your way with me!"

"Really, really no!"

The pout returned to her voice. "Doesn't the sight of my body excite you?"

"Strangely enough, no. Hm. Guess I really am gay. Sorry and all that. My goodness, look at the time. Guess you'll be wanting to go back to your room now and get some sleep. I know I'm pretty tired."

"Dammit, Patrick! Come out here and ride me like a wave!"

"I didn't bring my swimming trunks. Honestly, Cicely, I'm not interested. Go away!"

"I can see," she said, "that I'm going to have to take the initiative."

"What, coming to my room and depositing yourself *au naturel* in my bed wasn't initiative enough?"

She was quiet, I can tell you that. I hadn't even heard her slip out of bed and pad across to the closet. The first indication of imminent danger I had was the click of the doorknob, and then it was too late. Cicely flung the door open and then flung herself at me.

Fate and I were going to have a long talk if he kept throwing things like this my way.

I was still holding the bag containing wig and accessories, so at least there was something between me and naked female flesh, but I would have preferred something a little more substantial, such as the Taj Mahal or a sizable ocean. I let out a cry, a manly one I must point out, as she tried to smother me with kisses. Me being tall and her being short, most of the kisses ended up on my neck or chin, but still... pretty unpleasant. She seemed to have some octopus blood in her, as I swear she had more arms around me than a human normally possesses, or maybe they were just moving a lot. Then she put her arms around my neck and hoisted herself up, probably to get a better chance of her lips coming into contact with mine. When you see professional wrestlers in this position, they call it a bear hug. Although she was the one doing all the action, so technically it was hugging. Bare.

I wasn't quite sure what the protocol was when you had an unwanted, naked female attached to you like a barnacle, her legs wrapped tightly around your thighs. Frankly, it hadn't come up often in my life previous to that point. It could be argued that I panicked, and I won't dispute anyone who comes to this conclusion. I will just state that I acted quickly, and while it might not have been the most chivalrous solution to the situation, it worked. I bolted from the closet, Cicely still clinging on like a leech, and ran across the room until we hit the far wall.

With a loud "oomph" she slid off me, gasping for breath. She slid down the wall until she was a fleshy heap on the floor. I somehow managed to stay upright, and as Cicely had taken the brunt of the collision with the wall, I was relatively unscathed. She was definitely on the scathed side of the scale and let me know it. She let out an animal cry Tarzan would have been proud of and then began to scramble to her feet, her hands suddenly resembling the claws of a particularly angry lioness. The message was clear: she was no longer interested in making *amore* with yours truly. She would much rather rip my eyes out of their sockets.

Being fond of my eyes, I turned tail and fled. I was out the door and into the hall in no time, but the sounds of snarling and gnashing of teeth told me she was close behind. Not daring to look behind, I made for the stairs and took them two or three at a time. I reached the second floor and knew I'd put some distance between us, but I wasn't going to take any chances. Sooner or later, I would run out of stairs, and there was the possibility she'd catch up on the straightaway. I wasn't sure how good a runner Cicely Talbot was, but under the circumstances, I thought it best to assume she was pretty nimble on the old legs. Plus, there was also the possibility someone would hear the racket and come out to see what the fuss was all about, and with my luck, it would get back to Mr. Rivers. And that sort of thing doesn't look good on your employee review. I don't suppose there's much call for employers jotting down the phrase "Employee was once chased down the stairs by a nude guest," but it probably doesn't mean a raise is in the offing.

Hiding would be best, so I went to the closest door and threw myself inside. In the back of my mind, I must have had this planned, because I found I had my passkey in my hand at the ready without even realizing I'd fished it out.

I heard her growl as she hit the landing and then the thump of her footsteps as she continued on. There was a slight pause as she tried to decide if I had darted down the hallway or gone on down the stairs to the ground floor. She opted for the ground floor, and I breathed a sigh of relief as the sound of her feet slapping against the wooden steps retreated into the distance.

I leaned against the door for several moments, breathing heavily. My heart felt like it might explode at any moment, and, despite the coolness of the evening, there was a ring of perspiration across my brow.

It seemed to me something was amiss, and I quickly realized what it was—there was no one in the room asking me what the hell I was doing barging in as I'd done. As all the rooms were booked, I knew the room belonged to someone, and I thought a quick "Sorry. Being chased by a naked and very angry female" might be in order, but no words were needed. The room was darkened, but the television set was on, and I could see the bed, while rumpled, was unoccupied. Score. The occupant was elsewhere.

And then I heard a toilet flushing. In moments, someone would emerge and want to know why I was in their room, holding a paper bag. There was the rush of water, so whoever it was, was washing their hands. I had time to fling the door open again and return to the hallway, but what if Cicely, realizing I hadn't taken the last flight of stairs, retraced her footsteps and was now outside looking for me? Hell hath no fury like a woman scorned, the fellow said, and whoever this fellow was, he had hit the nail on the head. And I had not only scorned Cicely, I'd bashed her against a wall. Even your most temperate females will look askance at such behavior.

Still, I had to chance it. The sounds of sloshing water continued—the dude was really diligent when it came to personal hygiene—so I thought I'd make it. I quickly opened the door and peeked out into the corridor.

No Cicely, but I saw a large figure down the hall, coming my way. He didn't see me, but I clearly made out who it was: Gates Stumpenhorst. He was dressed, I assumed, for bed, wearing a tank top and sweat pants, and was padding about in his socked feet. Maybe he was working off some steam before retiring, taking a constitutional down the hallways of the inn before hitting the hay. Or maybe he thought he'd chance upon me out and about, just asking to be pummeled. Whatever he was doing, I wanted no part of it. I closed the door again, thanking my lucky stars I hadn't just wandered out without first checking.

However, I still had the room's occupant to deal with, and from the sounds of grunting and shuffling from within the bathroom, we'd soon be face to face. Maybe we'd have a good laugh over my predicament.

Or maybe he'd kick me out into the hall, right into the path of an oncoming Stumpenhorst.

So it was back to the closet for me. I moved swiftly, and I thought I wasn't going to make it, as I heard the bathroom door opening behind me, but the guy had been nice and left his closet door partially open, and being thin, it was an easy task for me to slip inside. Honestly, it was like an invitation. *Hey, come on in! Plenty of room in here, and no crazed women wanting to tear your eyes out or ex-boyfriends who want to stomp your spine!*

How the guy didn't see me, I don't know. Maybe he wasn't expecting to see skinny guys dashing through his room into his closet so he wasn't keeping his eyes peeled for this contingency, or maybe he was rubbing his eyes or something, but no exclamations of surprise were sounded, so as I settled into the shadows of the closet, I figured I was safe. I'd wait there until the guy fell asleep and then make my getaway.

I sighed. For an out and proud gayling, I was spending a heck of a lot of time in closets.

The guy walked across the room and sat on the bed. From my vantage point, I had a good view of the bed, and with the blue light

Rat Bastard

from the television washing over him I could see him pretty clearly. He was wearing tighty-whitey underwear, black socks, and nothing else. I cringed. It was bad enough to see some middle-aged guy in his skivvies and socks scratching his balls, but when the middle-aged guy is one's stepfather, it's really hard not to scream aloud.

Chapter Fifteen

JASPER K. Dollings was not only scratching his testicles, he was rubbing them. And not in a "Oh, I think I'll just adjust these suckers" kind of way. No, this was a "Hey, let's get these puppies excited" kind of rub. And then he let out a satisfied moan.

I cursed fate. Fate, on its part, wondered what the big deal was.

Me: I'm in a closet, about to see my evil stepfather wank his trouser snake!

Fate: But you're gay. Don't you guys like to see this sort of thing?

Me: *Not when it's my stepmonster!*

Fate: Well, it's too late now. Things have started to become aroused. You'll just have to brave it out.

Me: You hate me. What have I done to deserve this?

Fate:...

Me: Yeah, that's what I thought. Don't have an answer, do you, you bastard. Maybe I should have let Cicely claw out my eyes. Then I wouldn't have to watch this.

The stepmonster, meanwhile, had picked up the remote control for the TV and was settling back in bed. I couldn't see the picture on the television, but from the sounds of moaning and what sounded like skin slapping against skin it was obvious he was watching porn. I closed my eyes just as Dollings shoved his hand down into his underwear and began enjoying himself. There were some things a guy just shouldn't have to witness.

The film he was watching seemed to have only girls in it. It was, of course, a straight version of lesbian porn, lesbian porn made for straight guys. Lesbian porn made for lesbians would, presumably, involve them hitting Home Depot before heading out to the volleyball tournament. The movie Dollings was watching seemed to be populated by perky young coeds who couldn't wait for classes to get over so they could return to their dorm rooms and have slithery sex together. There was a lot of giggling and moaning and bad porn music. I bet not one of them was wearing a flannel shirt, even before the sex began. Lesbians, my ass.

"Oh, yeah," a male voice broke through the onscreen giggling. "Stick your fingers in there. That's the way!" It was my stepmonster. Shit, he was going to give a blow by blow description of the action in that husky "I'm pleasuring myself" voice. "Oh, yeah, spank that ass!"

Oh, for a cyanide pill!

The stepmonster let out a long, low moan, and I hoped he was finished. Tentatively, I opened one eye. I immediately regretted doing so, as he was still stroking his pud with his right hand. His left was alternating from pinching one of his nipples to massaging his balls. At that moment, I knew I'd never enjoy life again.

I tried to push the horror out of my head by concentrating on anger. Here was this holier-than-thou church-going homophobe masturbating to a bad porn film. Hypocrite! And he had the nerve to try to tell me my lifestyle was abhorrent! At least I was true to my own self and didn't have a weird, hidden life that included lesbian porn and muttering "Yeah, lick that thing" while jerking a— frankly—average-sized penis nestled in some really bushy pubic hair. Seriously, dude, manscape once in a while! Trim those suckers! If you can't see the snake because of the dense forest, prune some of them thar trees!

Although, from where I was standing, that was a good thing. The less I could see, the better.

"Get on top of her. Yeah!"

Lightning never strikes you when you really want it to. And it could strike him or me at that moment. I wasn't feeling picky.

I wondered what his fellow church members would think of his little performance. It was a shame they weren't in the closet instead of me.

A thought came to me. It was a slightly evil one. I dismissed it, but it did remind me that my cell phone was in my pocket. What with how fate was bashing me about the face and neck, it would be just my luck that Jake or someone would decide to call or text me, and my presence would be given away by the chirp of my phone. Slowly, quietly, I removed the phone from my pocket. A quick glance up told me my stepfather was too busy choking his chicken to notice a tiny bleep or two coming from his closet (and they wouldn't be heard over his groans in any case), so I pressed buttons to turn off the sound. And then, just for the hell of it, I pressed a few more buttons. It had a calming effect. Unfortunately, this didn't last too long, as Dollings suddenly paused in his penile administrations. The reason was soon apparent—the girls in the porn video were chatting merrily, obviously done with their frolicking for the moment. The conversation was banal and stilted (in other words, typical porn dialogue) and centered around someone named Cindy telling Doris and several other unnamed girls that she had to go do some shopping, as she needed a new dress. Why this would be a topic of conversation immediately after some major girl-on-girl action is a mystery, but I know few people who watch pornography for the scintillating dialogue.

The chatter didn't seem to be thrilling the stepmonster, who growled and began to feel around for the remote control. I groaned myself, inwardly of course, as I noted that his erection, previously so close to bursting, was losing its oomph and was wilting a bit. I didn't want to keep looking at the progress of his hard-on, but it was like a train wreck. Try as you might, your eyes just couldn't help but check things out now and again. Well, mine couldn't. I needed a police barricade and a nice officer saying "Nothing to see here!

Rat Bastard

Move along!" in the worst way. With the stepmonster's dick going the limp noodle, I'd have to wait for him to find another scene that got his libido going, and the whole process would begin all over again. It was more than a body could endure.

Dollings found the remote and soon found a scene to his liking. Cindy, it seemed, was becoming very friendly with the gal at the dress shop, and they were using one of the dressing rooms for some squelchy-squelchy. The stepmonster, pleased with Cindy's choice of dress shop workers, began to rev up the old tube snake again.

At this rate, I'd miss two inaugural addresses by new presidents before the bastard ejaculated.

I shifted uneasily, and the paper bag I was holding made a crinkling sound. It wasn't loud enough for Dollings to hear, but it did remind me that it was there, in my hot little hands. And suddenly I knew that bag and its contents were my salvation.

I couldn't just pop out of the closet and say, "Oh, sorry. Thought this was my room. Please continue" and then make for the door. There are things a mean, disgruntled stepfather will overlook and things a mean, disgruntled stepfather definitely won't, and watching him mold his penile Play-Doh was a big won't. But, I was in a supposedly haunted inn, and it was high time, in my opinion, that the Phantom Lady made another appearance. Anything to get out of that damned closet.

I don't know if you've ever tried to fish into a paper bag to get out a wig and underwear, strip your own clothes off, and don the said wig and gear without making much noise while standing in a dark, not very roomy closet. Possibly not. If this is something you haven't tried, I'm here to tell you it isn't easy. Even being careful, the bag crinkles. When you take off your belt, the metal bits insist on clinking together. And when you have your T-shirt up and nearly over your head, your elbow inevitably knocks against a clothes hanger behind you.

If Daddy Dollings heard any of this, he gave no indication. Maybe he thought it was merely extraneous sounds coming from the porn soundtrack. "Oh, Cindy, you make me so wet!" Crinkle of bag. "Yeah, that feels so good." Clink, clink. "Your tongue is magical!" Clank, clink, clink.

I figured that, with my luck, by the time I had the wig in place and was once again in the guise of the Phantom Lady old Dollings would be done and I'd have gone through all that for nothing. But once I had everything in place, he was still playing with himself. Christ, I could have ejaculated three or four times by then. In his defense, though, I must point out that Cindy and the dress shop girl's tryst didn't last very long, and the stepmonster had to pause to grab the remote again to find the next titillating tidbit of lesbian eroticism.

Before he even got a chance to find out what Cindy—what a scamp!—would be up to next, I burst out into the room, waving my arms and emitting a ghostly moan while trying to look like I was floating across the room. The effect was dramatic. The moonlight was coming in from the window, and I'm sure that added to the scene, but really, you don't need much to startle you when you're engaged in, shall we say, badgering the witness, annoying the Pope, or whatever phrase one likes to use for masturbation. Let's face it, by its nature it's a solitary occupation, and the sudden appearance of a willowy, half naked ghostly form floating across the room is bound to be profound. Dollings let out a yelp, followed by a string of cuss words I'm surprised he knew, and then moved. I don't know if he was trying to flip himself over to stand on the opposite side of the bed so as to have a nice bit of furniture between him and the specter, but whatever he was trying failed miserably. His legs did a sort of upsy-daisy, and then he basically went over like a sack of lead and ended up on the floor in a heap. There was a clunk as his head met up with the wall, but I didn't tarry to see if he was okay. With a ghostly "Woo-ooo" I was out the door and had it closed behind me faster than you can say Henry Wadsworth Longfellow. I had, naturally, rolled my jeans and T-shirt up and put them in the bag to take along with me. After all, it would give the game away if Dollings opened his closet and found them.

Rat Bastard

In the eerie light from the moon shining into the dim room, I'm sure my guise was convincing. In the bright light of the corridor, though, especially up close, one would not look at me and say, "Oh, the Phantom Lady." One would say "Why is Weasel wearing women's underwear?" and "Why is he carrying a paper bag?"

And, while Deputy Bradley, who for some reason was standing in the hallway at that moment, didn't actually say those words, you could tell he was thinking them.

Chapter Sixteen

HE EYED me suspiciously, running his beady little eyes up and down my bod. "What," he asked, "are you doing dressed like that?"

I tried to play it cool, as if everyone pranced around Inns dressed as a scantily clad female ghost and Bradley was the one out of the loop. "Like what?"

"You're wearing women's underwear."

"Yes, I am."

"Why?"

"Um... they're comfy."

"And the wig?"

I had to think about that for a moment. "It seemed to go with the outfit."

Bradley looked past me at the door, behind which we could hear thumps and curses as my stepmonster tried to stand and pursue the apparition he'd seen. From the sounds of it, he wasn't having much luck, but soon he'd get to his feet and would be in search of whoever had been in his closet, and I didn't want to be chin-wagging out in the corridor with Bradley when that happened.

"Strange," Bradley muttered. "Very strange."

I gave the deputy a haughty look. "Was there something you wanted? Because I have things to do. Places to be." Behind me in the room, there came a great crash, which sounded like Pop Dollings had upset a lamp in his attempts to get to his feet. There were muffled curses. I heard at least one shit, several damns, multiple hells, and something that sounded like flibbertigibbet. "Or," I added, striking a pose to show my indignation, "are you going to charge me with looking fabulous or something of the sort?"

He rubbed his chin. "I could run you in for indecent exposure." He didn't sound real sure of his ground there. The words came out slow, as if he were still pondering the legality of such an act as he was speaking.

"Nothing is exposed," I pointed out. I looked down. Well, something was *obvious*, but it wasn't exposed. The underwear was tight; what can I say?

Bradley conceded the point. "Just watch yourself, Weasley."

"Will do." These words were said on the go, as I distinctly heard footsteps behind me as the stepmonster approached the door. I pretty much sailed up the stairs. I had rounded the landing and was nearly at the top of the steps by the time I heard, far off, the door opening. Hightailing it to my room, I was so engrossed in my escape that I failed to notice someone standing just outside my door until I nearly collided with them. The person, hand raised and ready to rap on the wood, was just the person I wanted to see. Tony!

Tony's hand stopped several inches from actually making contact as I came up to him. His mouth fell open as he realized it was me. "What," he asked, "is going on now?"

"Long story," I said. I was slightly out of breath from the manic flight up the stairs. "I had to hide from a naked Cicely Talbot and I hid in my stepfather's closet, but he was engaged in jerking his meat so I had to get out of there so I disguised myself as the Phantom Lady and, well, here I am." I bit my lip. "I guess it wasn't really all that long a story."

Tony looked confused. "I see. I think. Cicely was naked?"

"To convert me. She wanted me to do some spelunking."

"And so you.... Never mind. You can explain it all to me in detail later, once you've got that stupid wig off."

I smiled. "Just the wig?"

A slight blush came to his cheeks. Really, he was going to have to get used to me and my life, or his cheeks were going to have a lot of dilated blood vessels. Tony even did that embarrassed, can't-look-at-you thing, and as he averted his eyes, I thought to myself that I'd really won the prize here. He was adorable. Now I just had to break through the Boyfriend Zone and make him mine. He indicated the paper bag. "What's in there?"

"My clothes, of course."

"Of course."

I closed the gap between us and put a hand under his chin. He let me guide his face up until we were nose to nose. And if you're nose to nose, you might as well go lip to lip. So we did. He put his arms around me as we kissed, and I must say his hands were nice and warm. The corridor would be classified as slightly chilly for a person fully dressed. For someone clad as I was, it was downright frigid. I would have liked a long, romantic kiss, but all too soon, Tony broke it off with a smile and an embarrassed chuckle.

"It's hard to take you seriously," he said, "dressed like that."

"Well, let's get into my room and I can slip into something more comfortable."

His cheeks became even redder, but he nodded. "Sounds good."

We were still entwined, swaying slightly in each other's arms. I knew I needed to release him in order to open the door, but my hands didn't want to obey. I didn't blame them. He felt fantastic. I leaned my face down and kissed him again. Just because.

This time it was one of those the-world-went-away kisses, where you're aware of the guy in your arms, his lips on yours, and not much else. It almost seemed as if we were melded together into one entity, and everything else was far away, so far it didn't matter. There was just Tony and his lips and his heart beating in time with mine and... someone bellowing.

Rat Bastard

The spell was broken, and I came up for air. The bellower was behind me, saying, in a big, booming voice, "Tony? Is that you? What the hell... who is that?"

I turned my head and, brushing a strand or two of the wig out of my face so I could get a proper view, looked to see who had so rudely interrupted us.

At the top of the steps stood Gates Stumpenhorst. I suddenly wished I hadn't looked. He glared first at Tony and then at me. His tiny brain was having a hard time comprehending what he was seeing, but finally he peered at me closely and realized I wasn't some tall, willowy girl but a tall, willowy me. His face went through a transformation, from questioning the scene before him to unbridled anger. I've seen angry faces before—my stepmonster's mug was pretty much fixed into an angry glare—but this one was a doozy. Heinrich Himmler, on being told that there was no milk for his tea because Josef Mengele forgot to go to the store, probably gave much the same look to the poor guy relating the message to him. And if Stumpenhorst's look of hatred wasn't enough to make me quake, the primal growl that escaped from his throat finished the trick.

"I'm going to pound the—"

There was more to this sentence, and I'm sure it was descriptive, but I didn't hang around to hear it. I extricated myself from Tony's arms and bolted. There was another, smaller staircase at the other end of the hall, just beyond Mr. Rivers's room, and I made for it as fast as my legs would take me—and when they want to show off, they do so.

"Wait!" I heard a yell behind me. Tony. He then added, "Gates! Stop it! Leave him alone!" Gates responded with something that sounded like "Garma sturmp hiss reggs rown ris froat!" which I later realized (once I'd had a chance to sit and run the phrase back through my mind under calmer circumstances) was "Going to stuff his legs down his throat," but in his haste to yell and grab hold of me at the same time, Stumpenhorst had bitten his own tongue. Really, it sucks to be him.

It's a shame the guys from the Olympic Games didn't see me dash down the stairs, because they would have given me a medal or at least a thumbs-up, seeing as how I barely hit any steps at all. I even vaulted over the railing to skip the second floor landing altogether, but I must admit it was pure fear that fueled this burst of athleticism. I was too aware, due to the pounding and thumping going on behind me that Stumpenhorst was in hot pursuit, and it sounded like he was gaining. There were still cries of "Stop!" from Tony, so I knew he was taking up the rear, but he wasn't really in the running. By the time I got down to the main floor, I was pretty sure he'd given up, and I hoped he'd gone to find a phone to call the police, several SWAT teams, the Navy SEALs, and Superman to deal with the raging Stumpenhorst.

I sailed through the lobby, where there were several guests, not to mention my boss at the front desk, engaged in chatting with Deputy Bradley. Apparently he'd been filling everyone in on his investigation of the town arsonist, and they were hanging on his every word. Why, I asked myself, did the Deputy and Mr. Rivers have to be friends? Everyone understandably looked up as I went past. I think there were even a few gasps from guests and a "What the hell?" from one guy. I didn't pause to see who was saying what, being too busy trying to save my skin. I really wished, as I made for the front door, that I'd taken off the bra at least, because it was pinching like hell. I made a mental note to write a strongly worded letter to the manufacturer of the brassiere if I lived through the experience and escaped the clutches of Stumpenhorst. Really, someone has to take a stand.

There were more cries of shock and bewilderment when Stumpenhorst pounded down the stairs and made his appearance in the lobby, but I had made the door by that time. I flung the door open and almost ran out, until I realized it was snowing. And we're not talking your lovely snowflakes gently falling to the ground, Andy Williams singing like a moron making a snowman snowing. This was the snow of an arctic god flexing his muscles and showing what he was really capable of. Loads of snow and very, very cold wind. I decided I wasn't dressed for it and closed the door rapidly.

Rat Bastard

The delay, however, gave Stumpenhorst his chance. He caught up with me, and doom was, figuratively speaking, written in the air. With a cry of success, he reached out just as I was turning around. I ducked, thinking he was throwing a punch. Instead, he was grasping. Probably wanting to hold me close to him to make sure he didn't waste any energy by having to extend his arm far to pummel me. Unfortunately for him, he didn't get anything but the wig I was wearing, which slipped off my head nicely. I hadn't had time in the stepmonster's closet to affix the thing properly with bobby pins and stuff, so one moment it was on my head and the next it was in Stumpenhorst's mitts. And I think for a second he thought he'd scalped me, because he looked at the wig in bewilderment. By the time understanding dawned on him, I had darted around him and was running back through the lobby.

"Is there something wrong, my boy?" Mr. Rivers asked as I went past.

"What's going on?" Deputy Bradley demanded.

I didn't bother answering either of them. There are times when you have to concentrate on escaping, and times when you can pause and give the bystanders the story, and this was a time for concentrating. There were other questions asked by the guests as I shoved through them, as a throng had decided to move closer to the stairs to get a better view of the madman chasing the young man in the bra and panties. "What is this?" someone asked. Mrs. Kendall's dog yapped, feeling that someone owed him an explanation for all the commotion.

I was heading up the stairs when I heard an angry roar behind me telling me that Stumpenhorst was finding the crowd that was now in his way an annoyance. I imagine there was some scattering involved—I mean, if you see a big, muscular goon frothing at the mouth coming your way, scattering is no doubt high on your list of things to do—but I didn't look back to check. Seeing Mr. Rivers had given me an idea, and I thought if I could reach the third floor without Stumpy getting his paws on me, I might not have to spend the rest of the night at the hospital, where some poor doctor would be examining my face, wondering where my nose had gotten to.

Stephen Osborne

As I ran, I felt with my left hand, and sure enough, my passkey was still where I'd put it, in the waistband of my panties (mine in the sense that I was wearing them). When I'd been donning the Phantom Lady garb, I'd almost left the passkey in my jeans, but something in the back of my mind had told me I might need it. Sometimes that voice in the back of your mind is spot on, and you know you should send it a thank-you card as soon as circumstances allow. Other times, like when it convinced me riding the Tilt-A-Whirl at the Winnebago County Fair after eating three corn dogs, an elephant ear, and two milk shakes was a good idea… not so much. Come to think of it, I should send my date that night, Adam Dean, an I'm-sorry card, even if it is a few years too late. He was wearing nice clothes too.

Timing was everything. I had to reach Mr. Rivers's room with just enough space between me and Stumpenhorst. If I had too much of a lead, he might look down and see the trip wire, and then I'd be stuck in a room with no chance of escape with a raging Stumpenhorst ready to make mincemeat of me. I'm a good runner and have energy for days, but it was obvious as we were heading up the last flight of stairs that Stumpenhorst, strong though he may be, wasn't in my class when it came to long-distance running. More of a sprinter, this Stumpenhorst. I allowed my pace to slow a little. Not so much that he'd suspect a trap. Just enough for him to get closer and think he was gaining.

I had the passkey in my hand as I rushed down the hallway. I could almost feel Stumpy's hot breath on the back of my neck as I came up to my boss's room. If I stumbled with the key, I was doomed. Luckily, adrenaline does amazing things, and it almost seemed like I was moving in slow motion—with Stumpenhorst moving in even slower motion, yelling, "I'vvvve goooot youuuuu!" in that sort of echoey, deep voice you hear when a cassette tape has fucked up.

Key in. Good. Run in, leaping easily over the trip wire. Good. Get enough distance in so the net wouldn't fall on me as well. Good. Sure I was safe, I turned so I could see the netting fall on a shocked Stumpenhorst.

Rat Bastard

He had stopped as well, but he didn't look shocked. Nor did he look like an animal trapped in a net, because it hadn't fallen. He looked evil and happy in equal degrees, and he was bunching his fists. I glanced behind him to see the trip wire was still in place.

"Damn it!" I yelled. I was exasperated, and I wanted it to show.

The vehemence of my outburst made Stumpenhorst pause. He'd drawn his right hand back to get maximum punching power but now held the fist in place. "What?"

I ignored him. I was steamed. "What," I ranted, "is the point of having a trap laid for a supposed ghost if you put the fucking trip wire so low that only a mouse using a walker would trip the damned thing? I mean, what's the point?" I had to throw something. There was one of those figurines of kids with really big eyes on the table next to me. I picked it up. He was soon to be a broken kid with really big eyes.

Gates Stumpenhorst seemed torn. On the one hand, standing right before him was the dude he wanted to pound to a pulp. On the other, said dude was behaving erratically, crazy even. And even big muscle guys pause before tangling with the insane. They bite. So he was hesitating, waiting to see just how off my rocker I was. He did, though, keep his fists clenched. No sense in relaxing them if they were going to be put into action once my rant was over.

"It's just stupid!" I yelled, throwing the figurine to the floor. It hit the hardwood floor and shattered satisfyingly. Even more satisfyingly, parts of it flew. And the headpiece became a projectile that shot toward the doorway, right between Stumpenhorst's legs. And it hit the trip wire.

I was shocked, as I hadn't been trying for that outcome, but my surprise was nothing compared to Stumpenhorst's when, seconds later, a large net fell from the ceiling and enveloped him.

"What the—?" he shouted as he tried to extricate himself from the snare. And, as any self-respecting fly caught in a web will tell you—or, for that matter, a super villain who's run afoul of Spider-Man—the one thing you don't want to do is flail around too much. It just makes the situation worse. Finding that throwing his arms around wasn't doing the trick, Stumpy decided to get his legs into the action, and that was his fatal mistake. He tottered as he got more entangled, and then—boom!—hit the floor hard. It had to hurt a bit, as he made the floor shake and rattled the bric-a-brac on Mr. Rivers's tables and over his mantelpiece.

I didn't stick around to extend my sympathies. I darted around Stumpenhorst and made for the door. He saw me making my exit and, with an enraged snarl, tried to reach out and grab my ankle as I went past. Thankfully the netting didn't allow him to succeed.

"It's been fun," I said once I was out in the hall.

Stumpenhorst shouted a reply. I didn't catch all of it, but part of it involved me doing something anatomically impossible to myself.

Chapter Seventeen

IT SEEMED like every guest and employee was down in the lobby. I was now back in my usual jeans and T-shirt, having stopped by my room to don—in record time, I might add—more suitable attire. Even though the Weasel frame was once again clothed as per normal, all eyes seemed to be on me as I came down the staircase, and they were staring like I had sprouted a third arm or was going to have one of them aliens spring out of me a la John Hurt.

There were lots of questions thrown at me, and the dog yelped, still wanting his explanation. Bradley was there, as was my stepmonster, Mr. Rivers, and Cicely, who was, thankfully, fully garbed. The one person I wanted to see among the throng, though, was absent. No sign of Tony. There were a lot of "what's going on" queries, but I ignored them all. While he was no genius, it wouldn't take Stumpenhorst long to disentangle himself, and I wanted to grab Tony, my jacket, and be down the road several miles by the time he got downstairs.

Mr. Rivers grabbed me by the elbow, asking me what I meant by staging a marathon through his inn. "And," he added, "your stepfather insists that there was a ghost in his room."

"Probably," I said. "But have you seen Tony?"

"Tony?"

"About this high, dark hair, face like a Botticelli angel."

The expression on Mr. Rivers's face made him look like he was on the verge of coming up with something, but this didn't help me much, as he normally bore that look. "I do believe," he said, stroking his chin, "that I did see someone matching that description. He seemed to think you were in some kind of danger, and as you had appeared just moments before he inquired about you, being chased by one of our guests, he may have been right in his assumption."

"Where is he now? Did you see where he went?"

Mr. Rivers shook the noggin. "No, I didn't. Or if I did, it didn't register. Pretty much the same thing."

Someone touched my elbow and, turning, I saw Donald or Darren—whichever twin it was—at my side. "He went outside," he said.

"In this weather?" Not that I doubted my friend's word. Well, maybe a little.

"He thought you were out there. Said he heard something by the side of the house and thought it was you."

"Not me, although—" I paused as someone upstairs let out a war cry, which was followed by the sound of what seemed to be a freight train tumbling down the stairs. In moments, Stumpenhorst would be upon me. "—I'm shortly going to be out there. See ya!"

I grabbed my hoodie from behind the front desk, where it normally resided with a stash of sundry items of mine I kept there in case of emergency, boredom, or just because I could. If I thought I could make a hasty exit, though, I was erroneous in that assumption. My way to the door was barred by the form of Jasper K. Dollings. Behind him was a very, very angry-looking Cicely Talbot.

"What," the stepmonster demanded, "is going on around here? First some weird figure jumps out of the wall in my room, and then I find you running like an idiot through—"

I tried to dodge around him, but Cicely moved into my path like an indignant queen on a chessboard who's ready to tell the black pawn he's got a lot of nerve thinking he could get away so easily. "You," she said, making sure the word dripped with contempt. "You threw me against the wall."

Rat Bastard

However true her statement, it didn't alter in the least the fact I had no time for explanations or apologies. If I couldn't get past them to the front door, I'd just have to leg it to the rear of the house and use the back way. "Sorry," I said. "Must dash!"

And, throwing one arm into my hoodie, I did my best imitation of a quarterback who finds himself with the football and suddenly realizes that his team has, for all intents and purposes, deserted him, leaving him to dodge several members of the opposing team who are frankly foaming at the mouth. There was a tumble behind me, the unmistakable sound of a large, muscular behemoth bolting down a flight of stairs. There were more gasps as the milling crowd wondered what new entertainments/disruptions (depending on whether they were enjoying the commotion or not) were coming their way. Some of them might have been aghast at seeing a tall, good-looking guy getting the stuffing beat out of him. Some of them—the ones who watched NASCAR for the wrecks and hockey for the fights—would no doubt have pointed out to Stumpenhorst that he'd left a patch of my skin unbruised and shouldn't leave a job undone, but I didn't want to stick around to find out.

I flew through the house to the back door, one arm in my hoodie. The rest of the garment flew behind me like an off-kilter Superman cape, although it was blue as opposed to red. The knowledge that a hoodie, even a nice, thick one like mine, would do little to battle the raging snowstorm going on outside wasn't upmost in my mind. Getting away was. And an extra layer of clothing would be better than nothing.

My hand was on the knob, and I was flinging the door wide when I realized I didn't hear sounds of pursuit. Stumpenhorst wasn't following me! Either he had given up the chase (unlikely), or he hadn't stopped to ask someone where the tall, incredibly good-looking guy he was pursuing had gone. With this in mind, I slowed my pace and took the time to get my hoodie on properly.

Not that it mattered much. It was still snowing, and the wind had kicked up something fierce. Snowflakes pelted my face as I went down the back steps, and it must be pointed out that these weren't soft, lovely snowflakes that made you want to catch them on your tongue. These were mini-ninja-throwing stars which threatened to rip the skin off your face and make your eyes sting. And there was enough snow covering the ground that, as I made my way around the house toward the parking area, my shoes and the bottoms of my jeans were snow-clogged in no time.

I was hugging myself tightly as I rounded the side of the house, thinking how nice and warm the inside of my car was going to feel and how I really, really didn't need the gods to throw any other obstacles my way, as I'd had enough for one evening, when I almost bumped into somebody. My first thought was that it was Tony. After all, he was out here somewhere, looking for me, or so Donald had said. But this figure wasn't Tony-sized. Taller by several inches in fact. More my height.

"Sorry," I said, as one does when almost bumping into somebody during a raging snowstorm.

The guy looked at me. It wasn't easy to make out features, with it being dark and with razor-like snowflakes pelting my eyeballs, but it seemed to me that the dude looked surprised, which made sense, as you don't expect much traffic by the side of a house during a storm, but there seemed to be a sense of guilt attached. Like I'd caught him at something he shouldn't be doing. It's the look a kid gives you when you walk in and his hand is in the cookie jar. Shock, yes, and his mind is racing, trying to come up with an explanation that won't get him a time-out in the corner, such as the cookie jar was choking and he was just trying to dislodge the obstruction. That's one I tried to use myself as a young 'un, and I'm here to tell you it doesn't work.

This guy had that look. It would have had to have been a great explanation too, since it was pretty obvious what he was doing, since he had a gas can in his hands and was in the process of splashing the side of the building with the flammable contents. If he'd had a neon sign around him reading ARSONIST it wouldn't have been more obvious.

Rat Bastard

He looked at me, slack-jawed. I looked at him, equally slack-jawed.

He was a young guy, maybe a year or two older than me, and I could see that, from a distance, he sort of resembled me. Whoever he was, he decided words weren't going to magically come to him and he'd better hoof it, and pronto.

Now, I'm not a violent guy. Ask anyone who knows me, and they'll tell you, "Weasel won't hurt a fly. A very nonviolent type, our Weasel." But everyone has their limits. I mean, this guy had caused me several headaches. Not only that, but he was attempting to set fire to the inn, the place where I was working and living. So something flipped the override switch in my brain that kept the violent tendencies at bay, and I grabbed the dude by the shoulder, spun him around, and punched him in the face.

You know how, on TV, guys are always punching each other willy-nilly, like it's the easiest thing in the world? Well, it's bunkum. It hurts, and not just the guy on the receiving end. Bare knuckles ramming against a bony chin causes a shock wave that shoots right down your arm. Immediately after the punch connected, I shouted—sorry, Aunt Matilda, but sometimes "shoot" and "darn it" just don't cut it—"Shit! Damn! Fuck!" and was clutching my hand first to my chest and then between my knees, all the while doing a little dance of pain. Which was a shame, because I totally missed the dude with the gas can going down like one of Mike Tyson's hapless opponents. Once the throbbing in my hand had abated a little, I did notice, with some pride, I must admit, that the arson guy was lying in the snow, out like a light. One-punch Weasel, that's me.

"Weasel?" a voice came out of the wind. "What's going on?"

What with the blowing and the stinging snowflakes and the punching the guy, I hadn't seen Tony coming around the corner of the house. He was wearing a nice, fluffy, down-filled coat and sported one of those furry hats that had flaps that came down over the ears. Seeing him made me feel happy, because I always liked seeing him, and cold, because I was wearing a freaking hoodie in a snowstorm and he looked fairly freaking warm.

"What's going on?" he repeated, looking from me to the guy sprawled out in the snow and then back at me. The gas can had flown from his hands when I punched him and was perched in a drift nearby, jutting up at an angle.

I paced and hopped a little more. It seemed to make my hand feel slightly better. "I'll tell you what's going on!" I may have sounded a little manic, but I couldn't help myself. "I was chased first by a naked, insane female and then by a steroid freak Arnold Schwarzenegger wannabe, and I saw my stepfather—my stepfather!—playing with himself! Did I mention that the girl was naked and that it was my stepfather? I did? Good, because those are key points as to why I've had enough of this day! All I wanted was to get some alone time with you so we could have sex before the Boyfriend Zone kicked in, but no!" At this point the guy in the snow decided to stir himself. He groaned and thought he was going to try to get to his feet. I leaned down and punched him again, right in the mouth. My hand objected strenuously to this abuse, and more clutching it to me and dancing about ensued. "Shit! Shit! Shit! And shit! Damn it all to heck, Daniel Craig never hurts his hand when 007 punches somebody! They ought to put up a warning during those movies. Don't try this at home, because it hurts like hell!"

The dude in the snow groaned something.

"Oh, shut up!" I yelled. "I've had enough of you! And then," I said to Tony, while holding my injured hand under my armpit in an attempt to ease the throbbing, "I come out here to make a getaway with you, and I find this guy trying to set fire to the house! And he's got one bony face, I can tell you! It's more than a body can bear!"

Tony was frowning. "The Boyfriend Zone?"

I stopped pacing and looked at him. "Really? All that, and that's what you picked out to question?" I wasn't angry, just puzzled. "Naked girls, the stepmonster rubbing his Wiener schnitzel, and a firebug, but you ponder over the Boyfriend Zone? Most people would have gone for something else, but okay. Not complaining, because it's important. But still."

Rat Bastard

Confused—and who can blame him?—Tony came up to me. He pulled my sore hand from under my armpit and kissed the knuckles. "Are you okay?"

"Been better, I must admit."

"This," he said, indicating the dude at our feet, "is the arsonist everyone's been looking for?"

"Presumably. He certainly was doing some dousing of the house with gasoline. I'm guessing lighting a match to it was going to be his next step."

Tony's eyes were wide—not easy, with the snow pelting us. "We need to get that sheriff out here! He's inside, talking to Mr. Rivers, and—"

Maybe it was my imagination, or maybe it was the wind, but I thought I could hear Stumpenhorst bounding around inside, going room to room in search of me. "Yeah, me going inside? Not happening. You go get him. I'll warm up the car."

Still, Tony hesitated. The dude making his own version of snow angels was moaning but didn't look like he was going anywhere, so I wasn't worried about the delay. "I'm hoping I get the whole story later, because I'm very confused."

"All will be revealed. First, though, we've got to get Deputy Bradley to apprehend his man, and then get out of Dodge. Once we've beaten the Boyfriend Zone, I'll explain."

"Yeah, about that." Tony put his arms around me, which I appreciated. I got some of the warmth from his coat, which was nice. It made me shiver a little less. "What exactly is the Boyfriend Zone?"

"In a nutshell, it's the time between meeting a potential boyfriend and having sex. Right away generally isn't a good thing, because then it becomes a one-night stand or fizzles too quickly. But wait too long, and you don't have a boyfriend, you have a boy friend. You've let things go too long, and the moment has passed. And I don't want that to happen."

"We've had sex!" Tony shouted.

The dude on the ground moaned.

"Shut up!" I told him. "We're talking here! That first time doesn't really count. Passion of the moment. It's the second go that has to destroy the Boyfriend Zone."

Tony smiled and kissed me briefly. "You're weird, but if this is something you really worry about—"

"It's a fact. You don't mess with the Boyfriend Zone."

"Then we'll nip that problem in the bud tonight. I'll get—"

He stopped, because our firebug was attempting to get to his feet again. I slipped out of Tony's arms and kicked him—not terribly hard, but hard enough to let him know he should stay put—in the side of his head. Kicking was much better than punching. My foot, clad in a nice, cushioned Nike basketball shoe, was much better at colliding with a human skull than my hand was. The dude went back down, and I'm pretty sure he was out cold. Good night, sweet prince, and all that. Gave him the ten count, because he wasn't moving. The way the snow was coming down, if we didn't get Bradley out here soon, he'd be Frosty the Snowman... if Frosty was in a fetal position.

I waited, hugging myself for warmth, over the still body while Tony rushed inside to fetch Deputy Bradley. Moments later he returned, accompanied not only by Bradley but Mr. Rivers. Bradley was frowning, which seemed to be the normal state for his face to be in, and my boss looked perplexed.

"Wombat," he said as he approached, "this young man says you've caught the arsonist."

"Seems like it."

Bradley, clearly not believing I'd done any such thing, leaned down and shifted the unconscious guy so he could get a better look at his face. "He's out cold," the deputy pronounced.

"I hit him a few times. Oh, and kicked him too. He wouldn't stay still."

Bradley looked up at me, the disbelief emanating off him like waves.

I shrugged. "It's been a bad night. What can I say?"

Mr. Rivers was staring at the arsonist. "I know this young man. He used to work here. Had your job, Wombat. His name escapes me at the moment, but I had to fire him. Not pleasant, but had to be done. You say he was trying to set the house on fire?"

I indicated the gas can. "He was dousing the side of the house when I came around the corner. That's when I punched him the first time."

Bradley grunted. "He's coming to."

"Adam!" Mr. Rivers exclaimed.

"Huh?" asked the groggy guy in the snow.

"Just remembered your name," Mr. Rivers said. "Came to me. Knew it would, eventually."

Bradley was helping Adam get to his feet, and I noticed the glare from some flashing red lights as a vehicle pulled into the parking lot. I couldn't see the car, what with the house being in the way, but I assumed it was a patrol car.

"You called for backup?" I asked Bradley.

"Actually," he said, "that will be the ambulance we called for the guy that tumbled down the stairs."

"What?"

Mr. Rivers nodded. "The big guy. The one that had been chasing you. He came flying down the steps, half covered by a net. I think he'd somehow gone into my room and got caught in my trap, the one I set for the ghost. Silly, of course. He should have known you don't run downstairs when you've got a net still stuck to bits of you. Bound to fall. Hit his head going down, poor sod. We thought we'd better get him to a hospital and have him checked out, although he seemed to have a pretty thick skull. Can't imagine he's too badly hurt."

Tony sidled up beside me. Putting a hand in mine, he said, "I guess that getaway isn't too urgent now, is it?"

Wow, his hand felt warm. My teeth were chattering, and I realized there were bits of skin I couldn't feel any longer. Going inside sounded wonderful, but I still hesitated.

"There's still Cicely in there, and she didn't look happy when last I saw her. And my stepfather! And…. Screw it. I'm cold. Let's go in the back way. Maybe we can avoid them by going upstairs the back way."

Bradley told me I'd have to come to the station in the morning to give a statement, but that, for now, he was going to haul Adam in for questioning. He still didn't seem convinced I was entirely innocent until Adam was on his feet. The dude shook the last vestiges of unconsciousness from his head and seemed to be slowly figuring out that he'd been nabbed. He glared angrily at Bradley, but the look he gave Mr. Rivers was murderous.

"You!" he shouted. "You bastard! You doddering old fool, you can't fire me!" He tried to rush at Mr. Rivers, but the deputy held him in place.

"We'll have none of that, now!" Bradley snarled at him. He then looked at me, almost like one human being to another. "We'll get your statement later. You'd better get inside for now. You look like you're freezing. And… thanks."

The thanks was grudging, but I didn't care. Not wanting to waste any more time standing around risking pneumonia, I grabbed Tony and led him around to the back entrance. After stamping the snow off our shoes, we quickly made our way to the back stairs. We paused there, as the voices coming from the lobby were loud and clear.

"The boy is insane. Must be. Running around like that!"

"Arf!" was Rodney's contribution to the conversation.

"The big guy really did a tumble, though. It's a wonder he didn't break his neck."

And more along those lines. I glanced at Tony, and we both smiled as we started up the steps. We didn't get far before I heard a voice behind us.

Rat Bastard

"Patrick Carrington Weasley!"

It was, of course, my stepmonster. He must have been lying in wait for me and heard our tread, soft though it was, on the stairs. He came around the corner, his face red and the veins in his neck threatening to burst. Tony and I both froze, me with my left foot mere inches from the third step up. I turned, inwardly cursing myself for pausing to listen to the hubbub from the lobby. If we'd gone straight up, quiet as mice, the stepmonster might not have caught us. As it was, his wrath would have to be faced, so I tried my best for nonchalance.

"Did you wish to speak with me? Because if not, we have places to go."

My stepfather's lip went into sneer mode. "You're not going anywhere! I want to talk with you!"

I turned to Tony. "Go on up and wait in my room. I'll be there shortly."

Tony hesitated. It was that old Lot's wife thing with the pillar of salt. Once the voice of doom has rendered your limbs inoperative, it's hard to get them moving again. Dollings didn't seem to care if Tony was there or not, as he went on.

"I've been speaking with Cicely."

"Oh? How is she?"

"She said you threw her against a wall."

"Well, true. But I panicked. I'm not used to having naked females throw themselves on me. I'll apologize when I see her. Tried to earlier, but she was attempting to claw my eyes out."

"She also informed me that under no circumstances would she allow her book to be published by my firm."

I nodded and tried to look sympathetic. "That sucks. But still. I'm sure there are lots of other, equally dull books you can publish."

The sneer almost turned into an evil smile, but only almost. "Since Cicely's book was the only thing keeping me from taking away your car and allowance, there's nothing to stop me from making your life hell. Unless you want to give up your decadent lifestyle and live in a way that doesn't disgust me, you can consider yourself cut off." He couldn't help himself. The smile broke out. "I'm so glad I didn't sign anything to keep me from doing this."

"Sounds like blackmail. Live like I want you to live or lose your car and money."

"Call it what you will. From this moment on—" Here he stopped, mouth agape.

I had pulled my cell phone out of my pocket and pressed the appropriate buttons to start the little video I'd taken up in the stepmonster's room. I had the phone turned so he could see it, and what he saw made his red face turn immediately white. "The picture quality isn't the best, but you can certainly tell it's you. Shame I couldn't get the TV picture in there, but the soundtrack can be heard, so one knows what you were watching. I wonder if the pastor of that hate group you call a church would like to see this."

Dollings's mouth worked a bit, but no words came out. He reached out, and for a moment I thought he was foolishly trying to pluck the phone from my hands, but he was merely grabbing the stair railing to keep himself from swaying. Finally he said, "You wouldn't." His voice sounded weak.

"I would."

"That's blackmail!"

"Call it what you will," I said. "Normally I wouldn't stoop to your level, but you've left me no alternative." The short video had ended. "Do you want to see it again?"

"You… you… you." The stepmonster wiped some sweat from his brow. "You have to erase that!"

"I will, once you sign an agreement stating that my allowance will be kept in place, the car gets signed over in my name, and that my schooling continues to be paid for."

I'll say this for Dollings—he knew when to cave. "I'll sign anything! Just erase that video!"

"Once the ink has dried, I'll erase it right in front of you so you know it's gone."

His eyes narrowed. "It was you in the closet. I thought it was a ghost!"

"Woo-ooo," I said. I then turned to Tony. "Let's go upstairs. I think we have unfinished business to attend to."

We went on up the stairs, leaving Daddy Dollings mopping his face with a handkerchief.

The chat with the stepmonster had allowed my fingers to thaw out somewhat, and by the time we'd reached the third-floor hall, I almost felt like I might not die from having all my extremities drop off from frostbite. We stood before my door, and I fumbled for my key, my fingers not wanting to work enough to get into my pockets.

Tired of waiting, Tony leaned in and kissed me gently on the lips. "You don't have to worry about any Boyfriend Zone with me," he said, "but if it'll help you feel better, we can get that out of the way ASAP. I, for one, am not worried."

I gave up on getting the key out for a moment and hugged him close to me. "I'm not good at this boyfriend thing," I admitted. "I always went from guy to guy before. Guess I was just waiting for you."

We kissed, and I felt warmth coming back into my bones. Sure, it may have been from the central heating of the house, but I like to think Tony's kiss had something to do with it. He giggled a bit as we broke away from each other.

"You really saw your stepfather naked?"

I winced. "Don't remind me. I may have to scrub out my brain to remove those images."

"And how did Gates end up getting caught in a net?"

"Do you want the story first," I asked, getting the key out with only slightly numb fingers and managing somehow to get it into the keyhole, "or later, after we've made love three or four times?"

"Later," Tony said. "Definitely later."

I was about to open my door when something down the hall caught my eye. It was smallish, dark, and was keeping close to the wall. "Hold on," I said. "I think I just solved Mr. Rivers's ghost problem."

"What?"

"He's been missing items. Keys, his watch. Little shiny objects. He thought the Phantom Lady was pilfering from him, although why a ghost would want watches and stuff is a question I have no answer for. Well, I know where they've gone."

Tony followed behind me, and I crept down the hall. The tiny figure had vanished behind a small ornamental table against the wall. I moved the table aside, and sure enough there was a hole in the plaster.

"Mr. Rivers," I said, "has rats. Or at least one rat. I saw it out of the corner of my eye as we were kissing. It had something in its mouth. Must like shiny objects."

I put the table back, and we went to my room. Tony started to take off his shirt, wanting to get to the good stuff right away, but I stopped him. "Before we do anything, I've got something to give you. Early Christmas present."

He smiled. "Oh?"

I went to the dresser to get the ring, feeling all warm and fuzzy until I noticed that the little box the ring had come in was already open. Open and empty. My heart sank. Someone had stolen the ring I'd bought for Tony! How could someone have gotten into my room? How could—

And then it dawned on me. I knew the shiny object the rat had had in his mouth looked familiar. I must have looked like a madman as I went past Tony and threw open the door. He followed me out into the hall, and before he could ask me what the hell I was doing, I'd moved the table and was down on the floor, reaching into the rathole.

"What are you doing?" Tony finally asked.

I felt something and got my fingers around it. Pulling it out, I realized it was a watch. Shoving the watch aside, I fished my hand back into the hole. "He's got your present," I said, grunting from the exertion.

"What?"

"The rat took your present. Rat bastard!" I muttered as my fingers found something else in the hole. Small. Hard. Round. I brought it out.

Tony's ring! I blew on it to get some fluff off. I twisted around, holding it aloft.

"Merry Christmas," I said.

Chapter Eighteen

I DISLIKE kissing and telling, so if you want details of the next few hours, I'm sorry to disappoint. Let's just say it was great. Tony was a lot of fun in the sack, and we explored and figured out what each other liked and didn't like—"Oh, no. You're not putting a finger there," and "Really? You're an armpit guy? Who'd have thunk it?" are phrases that sprang up—but suffice to say we smacked the Boyfriend Zone and made it our bitch. Oh, and we broke the bed, but I still maintain that it was shoddily made.

STEPHEN OSBORNE has been an improvisational comedian, a pizza restaurant manager, and a bookseller. Other than writing, his addictions include British television shows, reading mysteries, and (a recent addition) Broadway musicals. He lives in rural Illinois with Jadzia the One-Eyed Wonder Dog.

Visit him at Facebook: http://facebook.com/stephen.osborne2 and Twitter: http://twitter.com/southbendghosts. You can contact him at leftyIN@yahoo.com.

Pop Goes the Weasel from
STEPHEN OSBORNE

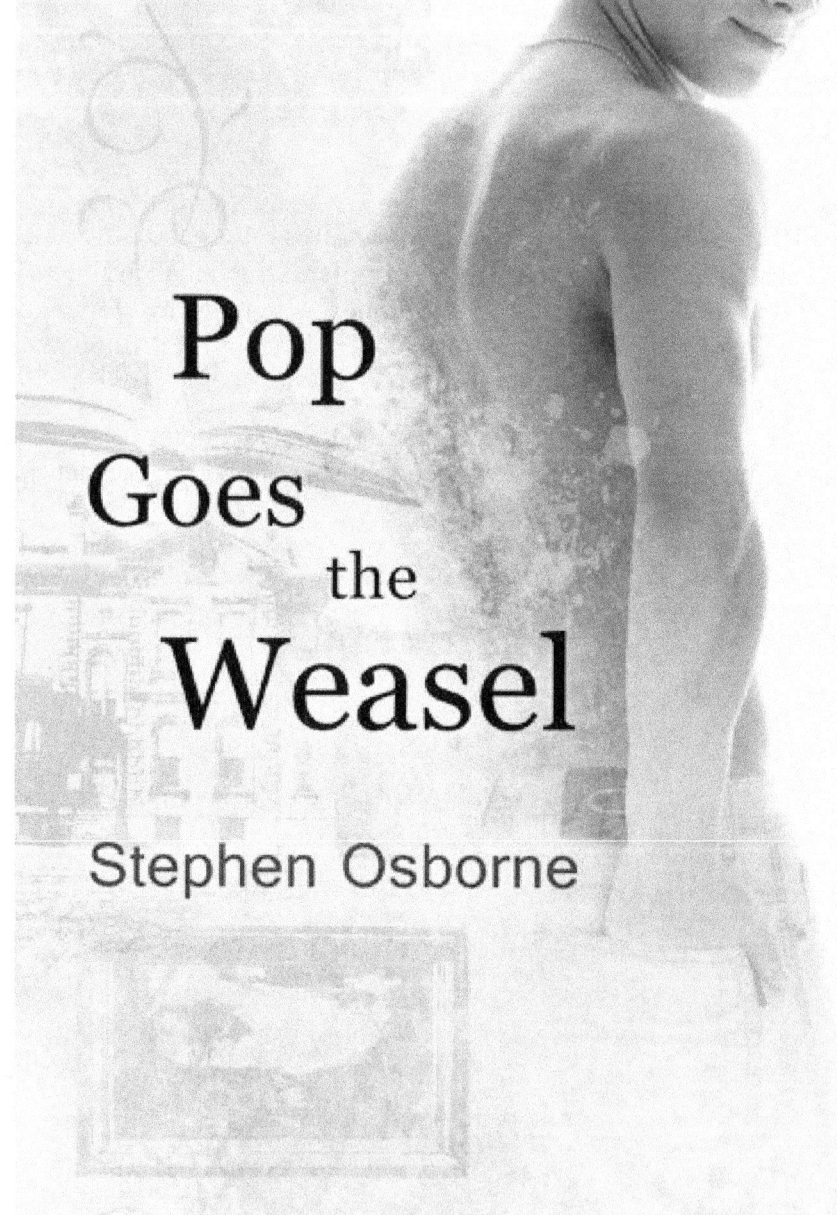

Pop
Goes
the
Weasel

Stephen Osborne

http://www.dreamspinnerpress.com

Duncan Andrews Thrillers from
STEPHEN OSBORNE

PALE AS A GHOST

STEPHEN OSBORNE

http://www.dreamspinnerpress.com

Duncan Andrews Thrillers from

STEPHEN OSBORNE

http://www.dreamspinnerpress.com

Duncan Andrews Thrillers from

Stephen Osborne

THE
SCARLET
TIDE

STEPHEN OSBORNE

http://www.dreamspinnerpress.com

Also from STEPHEN OSBORNE

http://www.dreamspinnerpress.com

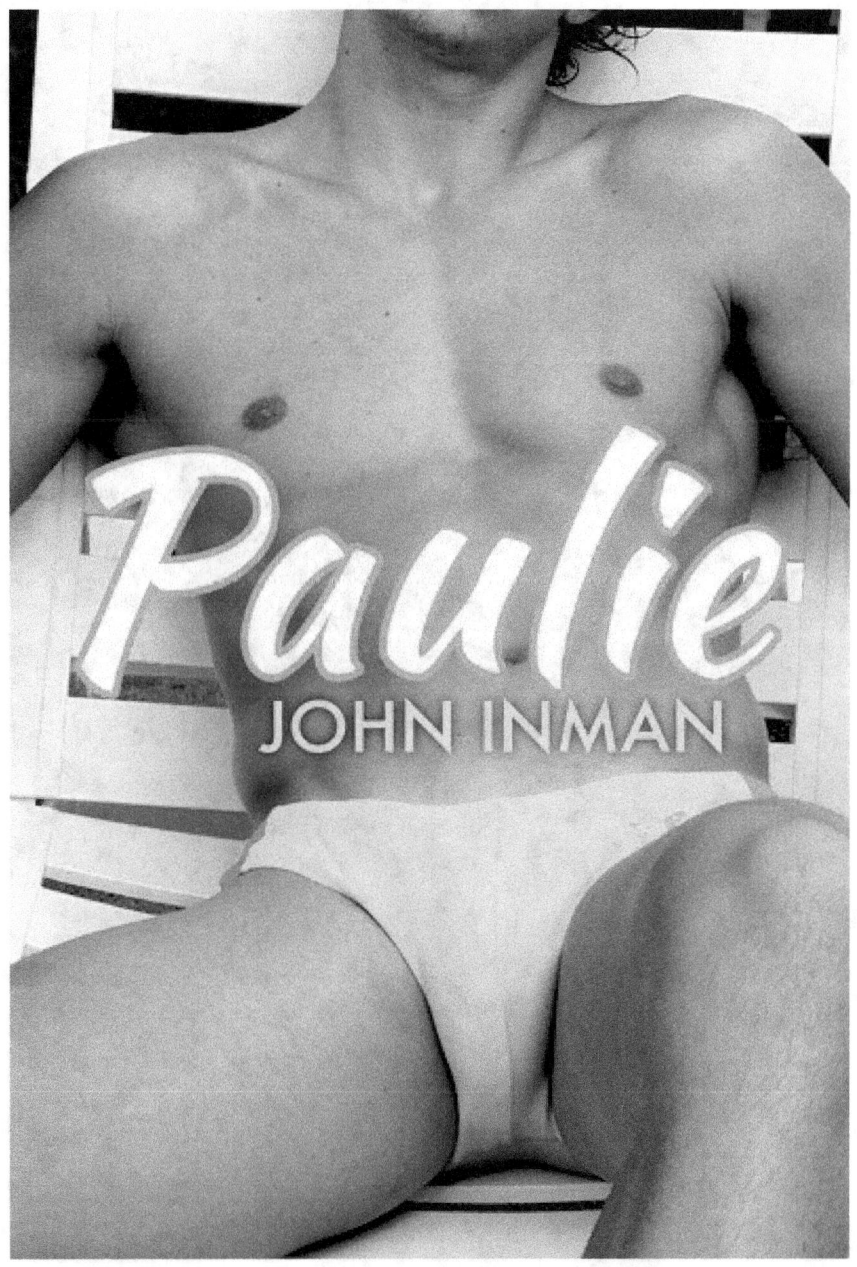

Also from DREAMSPINNER PRESS

FISH AND GHOSTS

RHYS FORD

http://www.dreamspinnerpress.com

Also from DREAMSPINNER PRESS

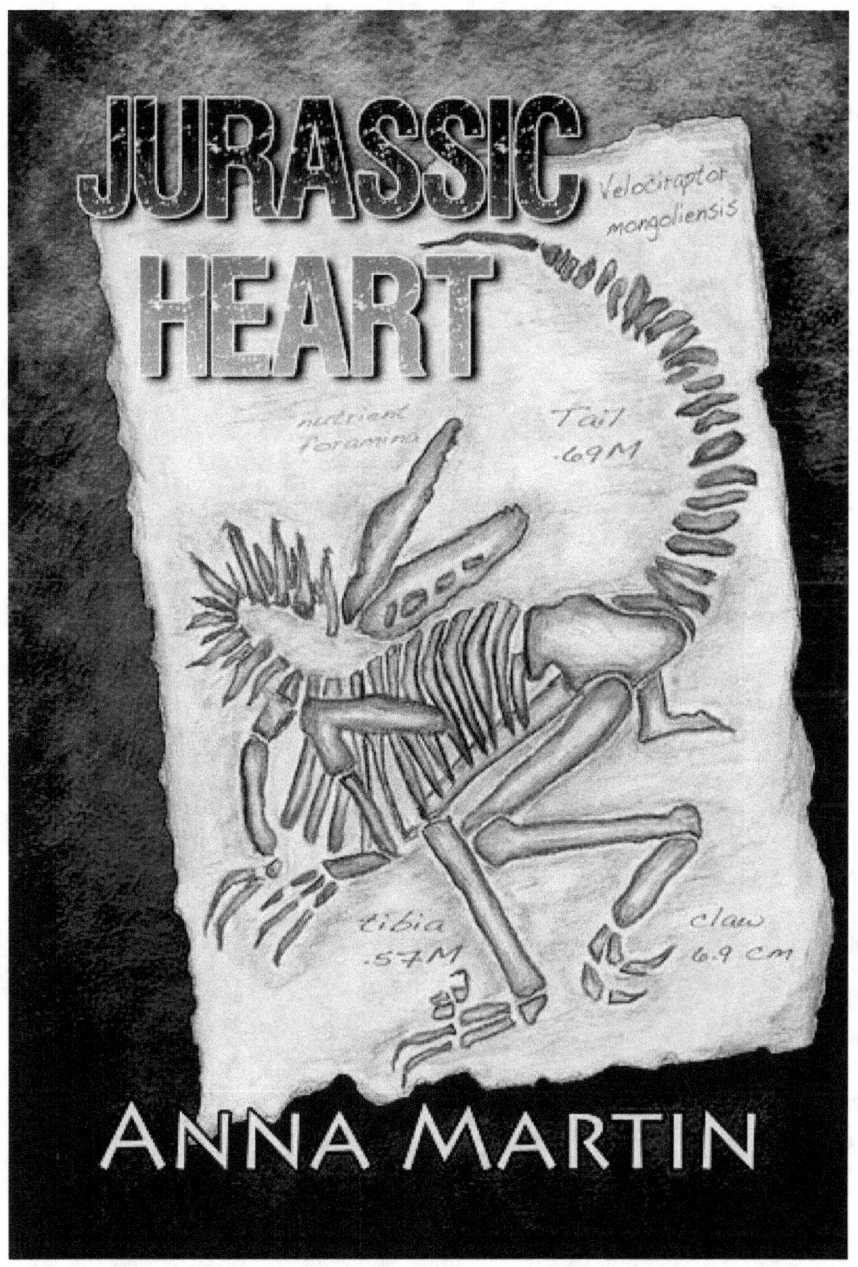